A DEBT FOR ROSALIE

Rosalie Garden arrives at Maldington House, an upmarket guest house, to work as a chef and earn enough to repay her father who bailed her out after her ex brought down her catering business. David Logie is the house's owner, and son of the proprietor Agnes. Still mourning the early death of his wife, David wants to sell his inheritance. Together with Agnes, Rosalie works hard to frustrate David's plans — and bring him to realise that he can love again . . .

Rosalie Garden arrives at Maldington House, an upmarket guest house, to work as a chef and earn enough to repay her father who bailed her out after her ex brought down her catering business. David Logie is the house's owner, and son of the proprietor Agnes. Still mourning the early death of his wife, David wants to sell his inheritance. Together with Agnes, Rosalie works hard to frustrate David's plans — and bring him to realise that he can love again . . .

ANNE STENHOUSE

◆

A DEBT FOR ROSALIE

Complete and Unabridged

LINFORD
Leicester

First published in Great Britain in 2020

First Linford Edition
published 2021

*A catalogue record for this book is available
from the British Library.*

ISBN 978–1–4448–4805–2

Published by
Ulverscroft Limited
Anstey, Leicestershire

Printed and bound in Great Britain by
TJ Books Ltd., Padstow, Cornwall

This book is printed on acid-free paper

1

Rosalie Garden slowed to a stop and set an exhausted foot on the ground for balance while she swung the other one over the bar of her ageing men's bicycle. Leaning forward across the handlebars, she was conscious of the ache in her buttocks and thighs. It was caused by hours of relentless cycling. You would think someone who cooked for a living might have more padding, she thought, and you'd be wrong. It was so easy in life to be wrong.

Rosalie straightened her spine. The fall from grace was behind her and mooching over it wasn't going to change a thing. She took a deep breath. Country air in the middle of a village had a lot of the stuff you breathed in in the middle of the city. It also had the powerful scent of azaleas in full bloom. Rosalie smiled.

She looked around the centre of Maldington and spied a small open-all-hours sort of shop. Newspapers and logs were openly advertised and as Rosalie moved closer pushing her bike, she could see the rows of small ads fixed to the door's large glass pane. There was a taxi run by Robbie and guaranteed to be on time and courteous. Rosalie pondered the idea of a courteous taxi and decided she liked it. Venison, frozen and fresh, could be had, together with a book of recipes sold to raise funds for the local Hospice.

'All in all,' she said to no-one in particular, 'it looks as if Maldington is an okay community.' She propped her bike back on its attached rest, checked its customary wobble as the device accommodated the weight of her two saddlebags before removing her hand and pushing the shop door inward. Seven or eight pairs of eyes turned in her direction, although a tallish man in a leather jacket kept his gaze on the front page of the Times Newspaper. It was yesterday's edition Rosalie knew because she recognised the headlines.

She stood patiently while the people ahead of her were served and noticed that nobody then left the shop. They all seemed to be absorbed in the recesses of the shelves, pointing things out to each other and discussing them in amateur dramatic type voices. This is because of me, she thought. They all want to know what an unkempt stranger with a huge rucksack is doing in their village on a Monday morning. Soon enough, Rosalie arrived at the counter. She smiled.

'I think the gentleman is before me,' she said evenly, but the man in the leather jacket made no move to come forward and Rosalie wondered if he simply read the paper in the shop before putting it back and leaving.

'You're fine, lass,' the shopkeeper said, 'He'll be a while yet. I think there's cricket further in.'

'Cricket?' Rosalie murmured, 'Of course. England lost the second day of the Test. I'm just looking for a wee bit of help. I need to get to Maldington House. Could you point me in the right direction, please? The signs have become a bit blurred.'

'The signs. Ah, that'll be the rain. Are you Mrs Logie's new cook, then? Only she said yesterday she was expecting somebody.' The shopkeeper smiled and Rosalie was aware of a few whispers behind her.

'England lost?' The silent man had a great voice once he found it. It was velvety but with an air of confidence and authority. Like everyone else in the place, Rosalie looked round.

She was startled by the intensity of his gaze and felt a tiny flush of heat catch her unawares. Light-headedness threatened but she shifted her weight a little and took a deep breath. Oh dear, missing dinner again last night was possibly a cost-saving step too far, she thought. Especially as breakfast hadn't been more than an apple and the remains of yesterday's lunch roll.

'They did, but not by much. Sorry, I should have thought before blurting that out: you might like to find the score for yourself.'

'No big deal. I could have looked it

4

up online, I suppose. It's Miss Garden?' he paused, 'You are the new cook, aren't you?'

'I am.' Rosalie held out her hand which the man took in a brief clasp. 'I like to be called Rosalie.'

'That's a lovely name,' a woman said. She'd materialised from the back shop and Rosalie assumed she was the owner's wife. 'I'm Sadie, which is not quite so poetic, and this is Tam.'

'I'm no at a' poetic,' Tam added, 'But she hasn't traded me in after thirty-two years.' He stretched a hand across the counter and Rosalie saw the other man drop some coins into it. 'Thank you, Mr Logie. I think you'll be showing the lass how to find the house?'

'I can do better than that, Tam. I just collected the motor from the garage.' He turned back to Rosalie. 'I'll give you a lift, Rosalie. Let me get that rucksack for you.'

'Thank you,' she said and was grateful to ease the heavy load from her shoulders. 'But I do have my bike with me.

I'll just follow along whichever path you take.'

'A bike?' Mr Logie raised dark brows in puzzlement, 'The nearest railhead is Wolcester.'

'I cycled up from Newcastle, in fact. Most of the way yesterday and the rest this morning.' Rosalie was conscious of the deepening silence as the other listeners absorbed this information. Newcastle was a good distance away and might seem even further when folk saw the amount of luggage she'd brought.

'Well,' Sadie said, 'You'll be very fit.'

Outside, Rosalie spotted an enormous Range Rover. Being a deep red, it was difficult to miss. Mr Logie may affect the strong silent guise, but evidently, he liked his car to make a statement.

'It's very red.'

'Easier to find at agricultural shows,' he said and threw open the boot to stash Rosalie's rucksack. 'Where's your bike? There's only that old . . . ' He stopped mid-sentence, and Rosalie wondered if it was good manners or astonishment.

'The old wreck is mine,' she said with as much calm as she could muster. Certainly, it was hers, but she was going to be so pleased to accept the keys of the promised estate vehicle that came with the job. It would allow her to come into the village and potter about the area in her spare time without blistering her behind.

'All the way from Newcastle?' Mr Logie said and Rosalie heard a touch of admiration in his tone. When she looked at her dad's old bike now, she thought she must have been mad. 'I wouldn't like to pry, Rosalie, but there is an argument for catching a train with this amount of luggage.'

'I know. Mad, isn't it? Which of the roads do I take to the house?' No way was she going to let him pry. The depth of her fall and the catastrophic extent of its consequences floated just below the surface of her consciousness but with luck would sink further as her new salary flowed into her new bank account. She moved towards the bike and stumbled as cramp threatened her right calf muscle. She put out a hand to steady herself and found it clasped in strong warm fingers.

'Take your time. The bike will go in the back. Can you walk?' When she nodded, he let go of her hand and Rosalie felt absurdly bereft. She limped round to the passenger door and climbed into the seat while he loaded her bike and its panniers.

'It's really my dad's, but he's had a hip replacement and wasn't going to be using it for a wee while,' Rosalie relented a little. That much personal information was hardly giving away too much.

Mr Logie settled onto the driver's seat and cast her a sideways glance tinged with more than a little amusement. Rosalie couldn't blame him. How often had she warned her dad of the dangers he was courting by refusing to buy a new bike and sticking with that ramshackle heap. Now, thanks to Rosalie's business failure, neither of them could afford a new bike and Rosalie quite simply couldn't afford her train fare.

It had been a straight choice between the fare or giving up the contract on her phone. She sighed. Not having a phone was the last thing she needed when in the jobs' market; and she was still in the jobs' market despite taking up her new position today. This post at Maldington House was temporary. Seven months tops her new employer had said. Seven months to lick her wounds, regain a little of the weight she'd lost and repay her darling dad as much of the bail-out finance as she could.

'Rosalie,' Mr Logie said and she thought maybe he'd already said something because the tone had just a trace of impatience.

'Sorry, I was daydreaming.'

'That's okay. I wondered whether you've done a residential post like the one mother's offering before?'

'Two, actually. I spent one of the summers while I was a catering student on the Outer Hebrides in a hunting lodge and the other one in a sailing school in the Greek islands.'

'Hmn! Quite different experiences I would think. Which did you prefer?'

'Yes, very different. The sailing school was family based with loads of buffets and a lot of struggling to keep the fridges and freezers cool enough in the heat. The Outer Hebrides was smaller parties of mainly blokes and too much heat was not a problem.' Rosalie laughed. A vision of a deep-frozen haunch of venison flashed across her inner eye. The intrepid hunters had had to have macaroni and cheese that night.

'Which did I prefer? I don't really know. The families were great although some of the children could be a bit fussy.' She tentatively straightened her right leg and was glad the pain had dropped to a manageable level.

'Some of mother's clients can be a might fussy, I'm afraid. She gets a lot of what I'd call over-the-top questions,' Mr Logie said.

'I know the sort of thing, Mr Logie. Were the beetroot grown in organic soil? Did the cow have a happy and contented life?'

'Was the produce handled by only vegans?'

'That's a new one,' Rosalie said with a grim laugh. 'Oh my! Tracking for the suppliers as well as the meat chain.'

Mr Logie grinned at last and Rosalie was pleased because she'd begun to wonder whether that tinge of amused surprise over her bike was as good as it got. She wished he'd laugh more often. The hard planes of his face softened considerably when he did. In fact, he was decidedly fit. Rosalie suppressed that reaction. Where had it come from when the man was her new boss's son and possibly, no probably, someone else's property.

'Here we are and there's Mother. She's been fretting herself silly over whether you'd come and whether you'd stay. I won't pretend to be in favour of her decision to keep trading, Rosalie, but for the present, I'd take a dim view of anyone who let her down.'

It was a body blow and Rosalie took a moment or two to absorb it. 'I may have made an unconventional arrival, Mr Logie, but my professional behaviour will not include abandoning your mother without a chef at any crucial moment.'

'That's all very well, Rosalie, but I do sense there are a few things you're not telling.' He was parking behind the house at the staff entrance so Rosalie hadn't yet seen the façade customers of The Country House Experience would have on arrival.

'I explained everything Mrs Logie asked . . .'

'Of course you did, but Mrs Logie is a trusting sort of soul and maybe the questions she asked aren't the ones I would have done, had I known she was holding the interviews.' He unclipped his seatbelt. 'Don't forget I own the property. My mother is my tenant.'

Rosalie studied the back of Logie's head as he slid from the car. She'd dealt with worse. She would deal with this. She had to repay her dad.

2

Agnes Logie, who was waiting in the back courtyard, was every bit as charming as Rosalie remembered from the day of her interview in Newcastle two weeks before. She was a smartly dressed woman, trim and energetic. Although Rosalie thought she might be in her early seventies, there was nothing diffident about her manner. Seeing her again, she could now also see Mr Logie's family resemblance. Both were tall with thickly curling auburn hair. She could also see the differences. While the son was slow to smile, his mother wasn't. She greeted Rosalie now with a huge grin and a warm handshake.

'My dear, I've been in a bit of a tizz wondering if someone as talented as you are was actually going to come and work in this backwater,' she said. Rosalie smiled back.

'It suits me perfectly, Mrs Logie. I'm really looking forward to cooking a fixed menu and just thinking about the quality ingredients this locality provides has given me loads of ideas.' A delicious smell wafted from the open door. 'Have you been making soup?' Rosalie's hunger returned to cause a low rumbling in her belly. She hoped the background noises of dogs and pheasants would cover it up.

'Yes, I have. I thought after your long train trip, you'd be hungry. It's cock-a-leekie. David is keen on prunes.' Mrs Logie stood to one side while her son emptied the car. When Rosalie's bike was set on the flags Mrs Logie made a small sound that might have been surprise.

'Rosalie didn't come by train, Mother,' David said baldly. 'She cycled.'

'From Newcastle? Oh, my dear, you'll want a shower before lunch then. Come through and I'll show you the rooms.'

★ ★ ★

David set the muddle of luggage down in the tiny hall outside Rosalie's rooms. He could hear the shower running and

14

thought Rosalie had probably left the bathroom door open so it wouldn't be a good idea to take the bags inside. He felt a tiny gurgle of laughter, unfamiliar and disorientating, swell in his diaphragm. Rosalie Garden was a very attractive young woman even if he felt she was holding back. He slipped down to the kitchen where his mother was turning a photograph around in her fingers.

'Nice looking man,' she said, setting the photo down on the island unit. 'It must have fallen out of Rosalie's back-pack.'

He glanced at the photograph and felt a stab of some emotion he hadn't experienced since Ginty Leodonis went to the sixth-year dance with his cousin Toby. Jealousy. He was feeling jealous over a ragamuffin scrap he'd met less than an hour ago. David shook his head.

'Mother, what do you know about this woman, exactly?'

'Exactly?' his mother repeated, but he wasn't fooled. She could play the poor little me to a tee when it suited her and clearly today it suited.

'Yes, exactly. Was she for instance the only candidate?' David could see the way his mother coloured under her usual immaculate make-up. 'Did you forget to insert the ad again until time was a bit on the short side?'

'If you know all the answers, my dear, why ask the questions? Yes, I did leave it a bit late and there are the Waughs coming this week for two nights with a small wedding party on Friday and Saturday.' His mother was defensive, and David felt a niggle of suspicion.

'Have you checked Rosalie's references? How do you know the woman isn't a criminal of some sort?' he blurted and knew it for the mistake it was instantly. Nothing would entrench his mother's opinions quite so quickly as having her people judgement questioned. Rosalie Garden came back into the room, but there was so little resemblance between the unkempt and exhausted waif he'd picked up and this composed, professional woman, he blinked.

Rosalie's hair was still wet from the shower, but she'd twisted it up into a knot and fixed it on top of her head. A few tendrils of light brown were straying around her long neck and they drew his gaze to her collarbone where it peeped out from the scoop neck of a smart red and blue checked tee-shirt. My, but the woman was thin. David realised instantly how thin and wondered if she'd been ill. As he studied her, he saw the way her complexion paled when she caught sight of the photo his mother had picked up.

'Rosalie, I found that on the floor. I think it must be your young man. You said you were an only child, like my David, so it's not your brother.' Agnes twinkled. His mother and her sisters like nothing better than a romance to gossip over. Perhaps if Rosalie had a boyfriend, they could plot over her and leave him be.

'No, he was my fiancé, but the relationship has been over for some months. I've no idea how the photo came to be in my packing.' Rosalie took the photo and folding it in half, to his mother's distress, stuffed it into a pocket. And that, thought David, is a lie. You very clearly do know how it came to be there and resent it.

* * *

Lunch passed off peaceably enough. Rosalie was pleasantly surprised by the delicious soup Mrs Logie had made and ate two big bowls of it with some toasted rolls.

'Like all function facilities, we always have piles of left-over bread,' Mrs Logie said. 'I find it's perfectly palatable if one warms it through.'

'Good,' Rosalie agreed. 'Otherwise, do you keep the house supplies separate from the function stuff, Mrs Logie?'

'Rosalie, David and Agnes will be fine. Tam insists on calling me 'Mr', but you won't find anyone else in the village who does,' David said with a trace of that impatience Rosalie was coming to expect. Who'd stolen his scone, she wondered.

18

'Oh, okay,' Rosalie smiled at her employer.

'The set-up, my dear,' Agnes said in response. 'Let's just toss this lot into the dishwasher and I'll give you a detailed tour. I tried to describe it in the job spec' but I don't suppose everything stuck on the day of the interview. You'd be nervous. I know I was.'

Rosalie laughed at this disarmingly honest admission but knew that David hadn't. He stood up and with a brief goodbye left them to it.

Agnes sighed deeply and when Rosalie raised an eyebrow, she said, 'He hates renting out the house.'

'Oh, is he particularly attached to it?'

'He was. Before he fell in love with Libby, he was full of plans for looking after his inheritance. I know it's too big for the two of us to live in on our own, but I don't want to be separated from my garden just yet; not while I can still grow a prize rhoddie. Besides, David is all of thirty — who's to say he won't re-marry? In my opinion, running it as a country house guest house is a good option.'

'You said he has a cottage in the grounds,' Rosalie prompted shamelessly. While she wondered who Libby was, she didn't feel she could ask about that outright despite the sinking feeling the mention of a woman gave her. Of course, she'd realised right away, someone as attractive as David Logie was bound to be spoken for. In any case, she had to concentrate on getting her finances into a healthier state, her heart could follow later.

'It's the old carriage house in fact. David is an architect and he converted it for his wedding. He stayed on there after Libby died, although we eat together most days. That suits us both.'

Libby was dead? The shock of that revelation kept Rosalie silent. She sensed it was still a tender subject and one that was affecting her new employer deeply. How long ago had it been, she wondered. It would certainly explain David's brusque manner. She felt a little embarrassed to have perhaps judged him too quickly.

'Libby was always going to die,' Agnes

said unexpectedly. 'She knew it and David did, too. Well, we all did. They were at school together when Libby was fit enough to attend, although they didn't get together as a couple until after David qualified and came home to set up his practice.' Agnes took a hanky from her apron pocket and blew her nose.

'You don't have to tell me this, Agnes. I'm sorry, though. I can see how much you loved her,' Rosalie said.

'Oh, I did, but there's other things, too. I would have loved a grandchild or two, but it became clear . . .'

'Of course,' Rosalie rescued Agnes before the other woman dissolved into tears. 'I think most of us hope for a new generation.'

'It's so selfish,' Agnes said sadly.

'It's natural,' Rosalie contradicted. She was surprised at how gentle she made that sound. Wasn't her own mother hounding her with no regard for realities over the lack of grandchildren. Her fingers closed over the crumpled photograph in her pocket. Why would anyone think having children with Steve was a good idea?

The complete tour of her new domain took nearly three hours and involved meeting the housekeeping staff, Betty and Wyn, and the kitchen porter, Keith, who'd come in specially to say hullo. The speciality seafood supplier called with a delivery and they all had a coffee together. Finally, Agnes explained how the numbers for the various keypads throughout the kitchen and stores were used as a security measure and what they were.

'Our outside doors are always open,' Agnes said. 'The house is so big, you'd never get from the Dewar suite to the kitchen before the postie had given up and gone, if you see what I mean. So, we leave the doors open in the daytime and callers can come and go.'

'I see the point, and the keypads are a great idea. Only you, me and Keith, can operate everything indoors from the ovens and storage fridges and freezers to the household supplies' cupboard. We add in Betty and Wyn for the staff fridges and household supplies and Betty's husband, Bob, for the garages and wood-sheds. Brilliant.' Rosalie was impressed. Theft could occasionally be a problem in professional kitchens, but in her experience, carelessness was a bigger one. There was nothing more demoralising than coming back to find a complicated dessert was melting because a fridge door had been left open. And with the guests unsupervised overnight, there was bound to be a few who thought finding a pizza and heating it up was a good idea.

'Brilliant,' she said again and tested out the numbers for good measure. 'So, my first assignment is Mr and Mrs Waugh and his Board of Directors with their other halves. Sixteen in total for two nights, arriving tomorrow?'

'That's it. And then from Friday, we have a small wedding party. Only nine of them. Imagine. We had two hundred at David's wedding.'

Rosalie reflected on that. 'I can't,' she said at last. 'Two hundred; really popular people.'

Agnes laughed. 'It's hard to exclude folk when you live in a rural area. Oh, and did I say, Mrs Waugh uses a wheelchair, so they won't be in the main dining-room. The table in the Peacock room is a much better fit for her.'

'Right. Are the Waughs in one of the ground floor bedrooms, too?'

'Yes. We do have a lift, but Mr Waugh says he's happier knowing he could just push his wife straight out if there was an emergency.' With that Rosalie realised these guests must be regulars who'd become friends.

* * *

Rosalie headed up to her rooms which were behind and above the kitchen wing. The house had a basement, but the working kitchen had been moved onto the ground floor and was large, modern and fitted with every gadget any cook might want. Everything she'd hoped for in the job was in place. What she had hoped to avoid, while living at a distance, was her mother's interference in her personal life. The photograph of Steve hadn't got into her packing by itself.

Once in her small sitting-room, she put on her phone and was relieved to see there was a signal. It would be good to have a little privacy from time to time. She kicked off her kitchen clogs and settled into the armchair. Her mum answered and was soon into a detailed description of her dad's first visit to the physio following his hip operation. Rosalie allowed her to chat because she knew how worried she'd been, and it was good to hear that her dad was trying to do the exercises.

'That's great, Mum. I'm glad he's giving it a go. Well, I got here okay and the job looks good. I'll be cooking for the family every day and the first lot of paying guests arrive tomorrow.' Rosalie paused while her mum told her dad she was okay.

'Dad is worried about you. He didn't think it was a great idea to go all that way on his old bike. Why didn't you ask

Steve to drive you up?' Although the engagement had been over for a year, Marie Garden tried to sound as if it was a temporary blip.

'As to Steve, Mum, the photograph you stuffed into my packing fell out and Mrs Logie found it. I had to explain a little . . .'

'It'll mean that son of hers won't get any ideas,' Marie said.

'How do you know she has a son?' Rosalie asked, diverted.

'Because they're photographed together in one of those glossy county magazines my dentist has. He's a divorcee.' Marie sounded triumphant. In her world view, divorce was a licence for all sorts of out-of-order behaviour.

'He's a widower, Mum. Look, it's over between me and Steve. He's an alcoholic.' Rosalie ran out of words as she did every time she contemplated the enormity of Steve's betrayal. Unfortunately, it allowed her mum to go on the offensive.

'Alcoholic! Really, Rosalie, where do

you get these ideas from? Steve told me himself he'd been working too hard and had maybe overindulged from time to time. Now that he's had treatment everything will get back to normal.'

'Mum, it's over. When did you have any kind of chat with Steve about it?'

'He phoned here last night. I told him you were away for an indefinite period, but not where you are.' Marie sounded regretful but not defensive and Rosalie took a deep breath.

'Thank you, Mum. Please don't. And please don't give him my new number either.'

'If you insist.' Rosalie smiled at her mother's long-suffering tone. 'Look your dad needs his tea. I am glad it's looking good, dear. Dad says we're okay. He's very keen that you know that.'

Rosalie drank the last of her coffee and let her head fall back onto the chair for a few moments. Dear Dad. Even when he was in huge discomfort, his thoughts were about her. Rosalie wondered how long her mother would be able to stop herself telling Steve where she was. Maybe he'd need two more phone calls to winkle it out? When he was sober, he could be very persuasive, and he'd always been clever enough to be sober when he visited her parents.

3

David headed off to Durham where his latest project was situated. He wanted to take a few more photographs of the rather difficult corner site before he sent off his draft plans to the customer. As he was negotiating the village main street, he spotted Tam striding out with a satchel across his shoulder. It was the shop's banking day.

'Tam, need a lift?' David called through his open window. 'Miss the bus?'

'Thanks Mr Logie. Aye, Mrs Hunter was in again arguing over whether she'd paid the paper bill or not and with one thing an' inither, I missed the bus. Thought I'd walk to Hangman's Hill to see if there was a car going into town.'

'Mrs Hunter? Are the family not helping her with that sort of thing? I heard Betty telling my mother she wasn't coping too well.' David put his foot down as they left the village boundary and the powerful car soon caught up with the bus.

'You could let me down ahead of it,' Tam said.

'Not at all, Tam. I'm bound for Durham today. I arranged it when I thought the new chef would need collecting from the station on my way back but, as you saw, she has her own transport.'

'Naw, I didna see the bicycle, but Sadie was working in the window when you loaded it into the motor. She said it was maybe a bit on the shoogly side to have brought the girl and all the bags from Newcastle.' Tam settled more comfortably, and David knew something else was coming. 'She's a bit on the fragile side for a chef, is she not?'

'She's certainly slim,' David agreed. No way was he being drawn into discussing the personal attributes of one of his mother's employees. 'Mother seems very pleased to have someone.'

'Good, good. We get a fair bit of spin-off business from the parties that take the house, I must say. Long may it continue.'

David wondered whether that remark was pointed or a simple statement of fact. He was keen to sell the house as he thought it a white elephant now that he was widowed without much prospect of children. In fact, he'd had an expression of interest from some folk who'd had a big win on the National Lottery. A picture of his mother's animated face as she discussed menus with Rosalie Garden earlier flashed into his head.

'You feeling the heat, Mr Logie? Will I wind down this window?' Tam's voice brought David's wandering thoughts back to the present.

'No, that's okay, Tam. Must be drinking too much coffee again. Always happens when a project is nearing completion.'

'Right,' Tam agreed. 'Our Nancy says exactly the same, when she's got a show ready for the curtain up.'

'She'll have one coming soon, won't she? I saw a flyer for a production of an Agatha Christie dramatisation last week.' Nancy Anscomb was the director of a small community theatre based in Wolcester.

'She has. Says it's been a bit of a nightmare trying to keep rehearsals on track because so many of the WI signed up for a garden trip to southern Italy. Anyway, I'm sure it'll be just as entertaining as usual and Sadie's hiring a minibus. Maybe your new cook would like to come?' Tam seemed pleased with this idea and David knew he was waiting for his reaction.

'Why not? I'll let her know it's happening. Which night?' He'd no idea whether Rosalie would be interested in community drama but there was no harm in asking, he thought.

'Next week, Tuesday.'

'Tuesday. Right, I'll let Rosalie know.'

* * *

Rosalie served dinner at half-past seven and was a little daunted by Agnes's low spirits. Possibly the older woman had meant it when she said she'd worried over whether Rosalie would honour the contract and was now suffering a reaction. Rosalie had thought at the time that her remark was meant to flatter.

'This casserole is delicious,' David said. 'I see you've been out in the kitchen garden.' He nodded to the jugs of herbs Rosalie had brought in and set on the wide windowsill.

'I have. I met Bob and he said I should pick whatever I wanted,' Rosalie said and knew it sounded defensive. Maybe she was also suffering a reaction because today had been a long day starting with a lot of cycling and the past months had been fraught with issues and difficulties.

'Of course,' David said, 'who has a better right to pick things in the kitchen garden than the cook? Did you have access to freshly grown produce where you were before?'

'No. I ran my own outside catering business, Dinners At Your Leisure, and it was based in a couple of industrial units on the outskirts of Newcastle. There wasn't an allotment attached, but I could source good quality stuff easily.' Rosalie kept her voice level and was pleased with the result. There were no choking tears as there had been when the business first collapsed and from time to time when another bill Steve hadn't paid floated to the surface.

She ran a finger around the edge of her plate and licked off the last ribbon of gravy. Realising how that might seem, she looked up to find David's gaze fixed on her. His expression was unreadable and as soon as he saw she'd caught him watching her, he hooded it.

'I've been living with my parents and Mum isn't the world's most adventurous cook,' she said.

'And she doesn't take advantage of having a chef in the house?' David asked.

'I think there's a touch of that thing about prophets in their own country. She likes what she likes, and she hates having anything in her kitchen moved out of place.' Rosalie softened her remark with a wide grin which Agnes at least responded to.

'Look my dears, this has been a tiring day for me. I wonder if you would both excuse me, and I'll head off for an early night?'

After Agnes left them, Rosalie and David lapsed into silence while they ate the pudding. David stretched in his chair and smiled. 'I'll have to watch my waistline if every meal is as good as this one, Chef.'

'I'll accept that as a compliment. I may not be up for much longer than your mum tonight. Cycling from Newcastle was a bit of an adventure.'

'Usually, I only eat dinner here,' David said, and Rosalie was conscious of a pang of disappointment, but she managed a smile.

'Your mum said. I'm to look out for notes under the dolphin.' She nodded towards the fridge magnet.

'Oh, by the way, I gave Tam Anscomb a lift — the newsagent. He asked me to mention an expedition to the community theatre in Wolcester next Tuesday evening. Tam and Sadie's elder girl runs the theatre. She's producing a melo-drama based on an Agatha Christie.'

Rosalie wasn't making much sense of this and she could see David sensed it.

'They're running a minibus so they said to tell you there'd be a seat and a ticket if you'd like. It would let you meet some local folk.'

Just as Rosalie did understand, so she realised how impossible it could be. She had one hundred pounds in her new bank and that was the minimum she needed to keep the account open. Apart from that, there were some loose coins in the outside pocket of her rucksack and one fiver in her make-up bag.

'Don't look so horror struck. The locals don't bite,' David said, and Rosa-lie tried to pull herself together.

'Sorry, of course. I'll think about it. It's really nice of them to ask me,' she gabbled to a stop.

David looked as if he was about to say something else, but in the end nodded and left.

Rosalie went slowly up to her rooms and when she was safely inside with the door of her little sitting-room closed, she allowed the tears to flow. Damn Steve and his 'illness'. What a luxury to be able to steal other people's livelihoods and then claim you couldn't help it. She brushed away the tears. Why should her ex get away with it? She knew now she'd allowed him to have too much control over everything in their lives and, as he was an accountant, to take charge of her financial affairs. She was back in the driving seat now. Maybe she wouldn't be able to go to this outing, but there would be others, and that was what she needed to focus on.

4

When Rosalie came down to the kitchen the next morning, Agnes was already there, and the smell of coffee crept round her heart.

'Oh my, but that smells so good, Agnes. I see you found the pudding from last night.' She tapped the code into the freezer keypad and took out several bags before crossing the big room to pour herself some of the coffee.

'I did,' Agnes said and blushed a guilty red. 'Rhubarb surely counts as a breakfast food, doesn't it?'

Rosalie nodded. 'It certainly does and there's no need to mention double cream, brown sugar or almond tuile biscuits.' She was confident her new employer wouldn't mind a bit of gentle ribbing.

'No need at all,' Agnes agreed. 'But I did see the bowl of real breakfast type rhubarb you've prepared.'

38

David appeared at the door. 'If mother is being a little bit dilatory this morning, you are working too hard. Sit down and eat your breakfast properly,' he ordered without any compensating grin.

Rosalie sat, startled into compliance by the mixed concern and authority in his tone. How long was it since anyone had bossed her around in a well-meant way? All Steve's admonitions had come with a sting attached. She wondered if this was what her friends with older brothers were referring to when they complained about them. Rosalie surprised herself by thinking she could get used to it.

It seemed David was breaking with his usual practice and eating breakfast with them. Agnes, who had been on the point of going upstairs to dress, changed her mind and sat down again.

'Later start for you, dear?' Agnes sent her son an enquiring glance. 'Only you were quite clear you needed to be away over to Highmere this morning.'

'I do and I will be going. I just wanted to make sure you were on track for the arrival of Rosalie's first guests.' David was pouring coffee as he spoke and Rosalie couldn't see his expression, however, she thought the words didn't ring true. They had a well-oiled machine here and, although things could go wrong, she didn't believe he was expecting any issues.

'Really,' Agnes said dryly. 'I think we are on track, as you put it. Rosalie is already working on the food and the terrible twins are coming in to set the table, serve and clear.' She stood up again and moved across to the house door. 'Personally, I think your nose was bothering you, and you came over to see Rosalie hadn't run off in the night. Given the warmth of your welcome yesterday, I wouldn't have been much surprised.'

Rosalie choked on her yogurt and had to get some water from the sink, but David seemed little phased by Agnes's outburst.

'Calm down, Mother, I had no worries about Rosalie abandoning you to cook dinner for sixteen with only Keith's help in peeling the spuds,' he said. He crossed the kitchen and held open the door while Agnes arranged the folds of her dressing-gown and steadied her coffee mug. 'Don't trip up the stair, please.'

'Try not to be too late back. You know how much Phemie Waugh likes to chat to you,' Agnes said and left them.

'Did you think I'd have gone in the night?' Rosalie asked in a small voice. Surely, she thought, she'd created more of a professional impression than that.

'Please, Rosalie, don't buy into mum's dramatics. Between her and the Doigs I often feel in need of a padded cell,' David said. 'It's a good thing Keith is so grounded.'

Rosalie finished her yogurt and waited as she was sure David had something else on his mind.

'No, I came across because I sensed you were upset last night. You don't seem to have problems meeting new people and I wondered whether . . . Well, I wondered if you'd like an advance of your salary?' He let the words drop into the

41

already charged atmosphere and Rosalie set her coffee mug down carefully.

'Why do you ask?'

'I looked you up,' he said. 'Online. So, I now know that your business, Dinners at your Leisure, wasn't it?'

Rosalie nodded.

'Closed abruptly about a year ago. I also looked up your Facebook page and discovered that a Steve Baxter, who used to feature on it a lot, looks like the bloke in the photo you dropped yesterday.'

'Ah, would you like me to leave, Mr Logie?' Although Rosalie spoke calmly, her heart was thundering. The blood pounded in her ears like a piston. Was the beginning of her recovery going to be cut down before it had properly started?

David shrugged impatiently. 'No, I would not like you to leave, although whether that will change after we have a frank discussion about it later in the week, I can't say. What I want to know is whether your reaction to the community play outing was prompted by being short of cash?'

Rosalie wanted to crawl away in embarrassment.

'I am very short of cash.' There, she'd said it. What would be the point in pursuing denial when she'd berated Steve for his lies?

David put his hand into the inside pocket of his jacket and pulled out an envelope which had her name on the front. 'I won't be back for dinner tonight. And don't call me Mr Logie. Please.' He put the envelope onto the table and left.

* * *

David slammed into his house. The worst frustration he'd suffered since Libby's treatment became palliative care, ate into his hard-won composure. Who was this woman to get under his defences and his skin?

How had he got the encounter so wrong?

He'd worked out a plan and abandoned it when he saw Rosalie working while she ate. Her slenderness was beyond the fragile Tam Anscomb had used to describe it yesterday, and it drove him to exasperation. Many people started businesses and many people fell by the wayside. There were any number of reasons, but when Rosalie's catering firm went under twelve months ago, she'd had a full order book. He'd found her website, Dinners at your Leisure, with little trouble. Its penultimate days showed Full stickers on many dates. Her business plan had been to take everything needed, from the food to the table napkins, into a person's house. Serve up delicious food and clear everything away as though kitchen elves had been and gone. Staring at her smiling face on his laptop now, he was puzzled, and he did not like being in the dark.

This was hopeless, he would have to winkle the truth out of Rosalie, but when he did interview her, he would stick to the plan and not embarrass the life out of the woman. Whatever had caused her fall, David had a gut feeling it wasn't her fault. Gut feelings, he thought, were no way to do business and he had to protect his mother's interests. Even so, the depth of defeat in Rosalie's eyes when he'd set that envelope on the kitchen table was going to haunt him for the next few hours.

How could he be so crass?

* * *

Rosalie was grateful her day was very busy. She could rely on Keith for basics like scrubbing potatoes, but without a sous-chef, everything was down to her until the terrible twins, Marcus and Mandy Doig, arrived in time to set the table and serve pre-dinner drinks. She hadn't imagined she'd be grateful for such total immersion on day one, but so it was.

She did run out of jobs in due course and just as she thought she'd have to let her mind tease David's discovery, her phone rang. Her eyes lit up when she read the incoming number.

'Hullo, Dad. How are you? How are the physio sessions going?'

'Rosalie, I was so glad when your mum said you'd got there safely. Is it really all right?' Rosalie heard the anxiety her dad couldn't quite keep out of his voice.

'It is really all right,' she said, suppressing the memory of her breakfast encounter with David Logie. 'Mrs Logie is delightful and she's very much looking forward to the visitors who arrive tonight. I think she knows them well because she's been invited to join them for dinner.'

'That's good to hear, pet. Listen, I wouldn't want to worry you, but I thought you should know. Steve Baxter was here last night. I was asleep and your mum didn't waken me. She knows what I think about that scoundrel.' Rosalie closed her eyes and tightened her grip on the phone.

'Do you know what he wanted?'

'Your mum is a bit vague. He brought her flowers, pink peonies of all things. Great blousy . . .'

46

'Yes, Steve would always go for something spectacular. I wonder how he could afford them?' Rosalie knew Steve was living on benefits and there would hardly be spare cash to buy flamboyant bunches of flowers.

'Good question, but a better one is what your mum might have let slip. She was very adamant she'd not said where you were, but I have a sneaky feeling I heard her saying 'Logie' as I woke up.' Roger Garden sounded angry but defeated at the same time. 'Listen, my dear, you don't have to repay all of the money I used to wind things up. Really, it would all be coming to you in any case.'

'Dad we've been through this. I need to repay the money. I cannot face myself knowing how straitened the loan is making life for you and mum,' Rosalie said gently.

'It just makes things a bit different. Your mum had to drive me to the physio. Imagine that. When was she last behind the wheel? She did okay, too. We maybe can't afford a taxi, but if we could we'd be saving pounds.'

Rosalie wasn't sure about the logic in there and her heart missed a beat when she heard about her mum driving.

'By the way, you do need a new bike,' she said, 'I don't think I'm even going to bring the current one back to Newcastle.'

'What! Oh, well, I suppose my bike riding days are over.'

'Nonsense, just over on that bone-shaker.' Rosalie spent a couple more minutes reassuring her dad before they hung up.

There was a quick rap on the kitchen door before it flew open and two smartly dressed young people came in. Rosalie stood up.

'You have to be . . .'

'The Terrible Twins,' they said together.

'Mandy,' the girl said.

'Marcus,' the boy said.

'Rosalie,' she said with a broad grin. 'I can't not say it. You two are so alike; I don't know how I'm going to tell you apart.'

'Does this help at all?' Mandy asked

as she turned sideways and set one hand on her hip while sending Rosalie a cheeky grin. Still slim from the side, she did nonetheless sport respectable womanly curves.

'Um! Of course, but from the back . . . '

'The back!' Marcus exclaimed in a theatrical voice. He turned away and sashayed across the kitchen floor narrowly missing a tray of glasses Rosalie had set out ready to fill with this evening's dessert. She took a huge breath and found Mandy's hand gripping her wrist.

'He never earns anything here, you know. Mrs L takes it all back in breakages.' Rosalie thought the girl had to be joking, but her serious expression and downcast gaze was very convincing.

'Mandy, don't scare our new chef away before she's even done one event for us, please,' Agnes said from the doorway. Rosalie watched in amusement as Marcus stopped his posing and went over to plant a kiss on Agnes's cheek.

'Hullo, Mrs L,' he said in a sultry undertone, 'Aren't you looking the

Grande Dame tonight? Mr Waugh bringing his business partner, is he?'

'Marcus, I don't know why I hire you two, I really don't.'

'You couldn't get anyone else to keep coming back for the wages, Mrs L,' Mandy said, and Rosalie still couldn't work out whether she was serious or not.

'Huh!' Agnes said, 'And where else around here would you get any work while waiting for the break-through part to break through?'

'We've got something, you know. Did David tell?' Marcus asked in what was possibly his own voice, but Rosalie couldn't be sure. His excitement was infectious and she held her breath waiting to hear what the part might be.

'No, he did not. In Newcastle?' Agnes came fully into the kitchen and Rosalie saw what Marcus meant when he'd commented on her outfit. She was wearing a knee-length dress decorated with large overlapping spangles on the skirt and smaller ones across the bodice and

50

sleeves. The midnight blue shade complimented her eyes and gave definition to her pale colouring. She did look rather special and was very definitely not going to be helping out in the kitchen. In fact, Rosalie looked round in case she and Keith had missed any spills the older woman might snag and stain the lovely gown with as she walked past.

'Curiously, it's here, at least in Wolcester,' Mandy said and clapped her hands. 'There's a small animation studio and it needs voices for a film that'll go out to lots of festivals. We'll be away all of next week, Mrs L. Is that a problem?'

'No, no. Next week is still free in the diary after the wedding at the weekend. You can do that, can't you?' Agnes asked without displaying much concern. Nine people probably didn't offer a big challenge even if the waiters were absent.

'So, are you both actors?' Rosalie asked.

'Didn't you guess?' Marcus asked lifting his gaze from Agnes to grin at her. 'We're in a constant state of 'resting' so working here suits us and suits Mrs L, bless her.' He winked at Agnes before taking a couple of aprons out of a drawer and throwing one to his twin.

'Resting,' Agnes said ten minutes later when the twins had headed off towards the Peacock dining-room with a laden trolley, 'But by no means restful.'

'They seem very pleasant, though.' Rosalie replied with one eye on the clock. She would soon have to begin the actual cooking of all the food now prepped and sitting around in the various fridges.

'They are nice young people and good to have about the place. They kept us sane when Libby died. They seemed to know instinctively when what you needed was a few minutes on your own or an in-depth discussion of the latest productions mentioned in The List.' Agnes shook her head. 'I suppose that's what a good actor needs to do, isn't it? Observe and store the observations.'

5

Rosalie was closing the final fridge after preparing a fruit salad for the breakfast buffet when the kitchen door opened and David came in. She stood and watched him wondering nervously whether he'd come over to discuss her business failure so soon.

'Your stare is a little unnerving. Do I have twigs in my hair?' It was such an unexpected question, Rosalie simply shook her head. 'Good. How did the first day go off? I think mum likes the Waughs a lot.' David looked around the kitchen as he spoke and the gesture made Rosalie wonder whether he'd eaten. He was a tall man and quite rangy. It would be a temptation to any girlfriend to feed him up, she was sure.

'Have you eaten?' she asked and immediately wondered why. Surely the less time she spent in David Logie's company, the better it would be for her peace of mind.

'Yes, I bought a pie and chips, although the pie was so greasy I threw half of it to the gulls,' he said. 'I should remember what will happen, but somehow I always think that the next one will be better.'

'Hmn!' Rosalie muttered. She opened the small fridge used by the household and surveyed the contents. 'Leftovers include half a portion of green soup and a fairly good slice of the braised venison the Waughs chose as their main course.'

'Is that an offer, Chef?'

'Sit down.' Rosalie soon had the food heated through and watched with satisfaction as David devoured the lot.

'Very good,' her employer's son said with an appreciative smile. He rose to clear his plates, but Rosalie took them from him and added them to the house dishwasher. 'Our most recent chef, before you rescued mum, was a middle-aged man from the Borders. He liked it here, but his parents had begun to need a bit more support than he could offer from such a distance.'

'Did he get another position?' Rosalie asked. Chefs did move around a lot. Cooking was a wonderfully mobile skill to be practised in.

'Three actually while he tried to make Mum believe he really had to move. One four months ago, another two weeks after that and then in exasperation, a third one. Mum, for all her entrepreneurial talent, can be inclined to hang on when things suit her.'

'Oh,' Rosalie replied, surprised as much by David's frankness as his overt criticism. 'I see. Head in the sand?'

'Sorry, I don't mean to dampen your spirits when it's all gone well. Yes, she can be a little inclined to ignore what doesn't suit her.' David glanced out of the window. 'There's still a lot of light in the sky. Would you like a walk? I can show you how to manage it without bumping into the guests.'

Rosalie laughed at that. Agnes had said how David didn't enjoy sharing the property and his offer seemed to back that up. 'Secret paths and underground tunnels?' she teased. 'I would like a walk. Give me a minute to get out of the uniform.' She dashed upstairs and stripped off her kitchen clothing. Replacing the shapeless trousers and double-breasted jacket with a light raspberry coloured sweater and khaki shorts, she pulled a brush through her curls and slipped on some deck shoes. They were robust enough to cope with grass but not too heavy for her tired legs and feet.

'There may be midges,' David said when she reappeared in the kitchen. Had she imagined the appreciative gleam of interest in his eyes when he took in the length of her legs? She had spent so much time recently riding around Newcastle on her dad's old bike trying to secure work, that they were toned and tanned.

'Really? Doesn't the breeze keep the midges at bay?' she asked as much to cover her confusion over his interest as to find out what the midges might be doing.

They left the house by a side entrance

off the service corridor leading to the front door. The air was heavy with the scent of azaleas and the tarragon that grew in the lawns. Rosalie began to think Maldington House was a wonderful refuge to have found. She felt David's hand gently in the small of her back as he steered her towards a small door in the curtain wall that protected the front porch. How long was it since she'd known the comfort of a warm hand helping her?

The wind was lively but not cold. She felt David tense as he breathed in the evening air. It must be hard sometimes to live with his accumulated memories, she thought.

She heard him shake out a bunch of keys and select one. The others fell onto the ring and she watched it swing back and forth as he opened the door. It slid back, and they stepped through onto a path concealed from the more public one to the kitchen garden by hawthorn hedging. Further along a pheasant let out an enraged squawk and leapt off the ground to crash through the hedge and disappear.

'I wonder if pheasants feel threatened when the chef comes out for a stroll?' David mused and Rosalie laughed again. There hadn't been much to lighten her mood over the recent past and even something small like whether a pheasant could recognise the local chef tickled her fancy.

David listened to Rosalie's appreciative chuckle. One of the worst things about living life as a singleton was not having anyone to share intimate moments of small stuff: like a pheasant worrying about the chef.

He knew she'd clocked his reaction to her legs and yet again wanted to kick himself. He was thirty and a widower for crying out loud. Anyone would think he'd never seen an attractive woman before and of course after Libby died, every woman in the district had resorted to flirting with him. It was a recognised thing apparently.

Well, he thought ruefully, Rosalie Garden wasn't flirting with him. She'd laughed all right, but he'd seen the way her shoulders tensed immediately. Was she reminding herself that he was by way of 'the enemy'? Telling her how his mum had held onto poor Dougie, could be taken as a warning that he still wanted to close down the paying guests' business and sell up.

The house and estate were beautiful but all-consuming. Maybe if Libby hadn't been so ill for so long, his energy would have come back more quickly after she died.

He watched the woman in front of him as she peered through the hedge where the pheasant had flapped to safety. Curiously, he'd felt a surge of his old proprietorial interest in the property over the last couple of days. It wouldn't do, though. He had the first of a few seriously interested prospective buyers arriving in the middle of the next week. Rosalie Garden's attractiveness was an unwelcome and unwanted distraction.

* * *

Having been out with David around the policies in the quiet of the night, Rosalie was tempted to make another tour the following morning. She'd arrived into the back yard with David on the day she started work and hadn't had the opportunity to take a look at the house's frontage. The pictures posted on the business website made it look very attractive indeed. Rosalie was looking forward to seeing it while she could smell the gardens all around, too.

She'd cleared up after breakfast and was confident the arrangements for lunch were under control, so thought a wander around the front of the house would be good. As far as she knew, the whole group was occupied in the house's small conference room undertaking an elaborate team-building exercise.

Rosalie swapped her kitchen tunic for a lightweight tracksuit, her clogs for deck shoes and let herself out through the back yard. The dogs weren't in the kennels, but she caught sight of one or two of them snuffling around in the policies where Bob's lawnmower could be heard. A large Irish Setter merged from some shrubbery and would have come over to investigate Rosalie, had a whistle not sounded just then. The dog hesitated but looked around and decided its best interests lay with the pack. Rosalie watched it pick up speed and disappear around the end of the carriage house.

'They are so very well trained,' a woman said, and Rosalie looked around and then down. Mrs Waugh was watching the setter's red coat wave in the sunlight. She'd approached across some short grass and stopped her chair just out of Rosalie's eyeline.

'Good morning, Mrs Waugh,' Rosalie said, 'I thought everyone was in the conference room. Can I get you anything — a cup of coffee?'

'No, nothing, thank you. You're feeding and watering us every bit as well as Dougie did. I told Reuben I wouldn't take part in this morning's session but take the chance of the sun while it was shining.' She threw her head back and gazed briefly into the sky.

'I was just going to have a wander around the front of the house,' Rosalie said, 'But I can go on another occasion.'

'Good gracious, my dear, that's a very feudal attitude. Why don't we go together?' Phemie Waugh set her electric chair in motion and Rosalie followed her.

The house was mid-Victorian and probably built in the heyday of Country House construction by the architect, David Bryce. She'd heard one of the party say the round towers were a Bryce trademark and resolved to ask David later.

'It's a Bryce house,' David said behind them. Phemie Waugh craned her head round and Rosalie made a tiny startled jump. My goodness, she thought, am I conjuring this man now. 'He didn't do much work like this outside Scotland, but it's definitely by him. Dad found the drawings, letters and even some of the bills.'

'David, my dear. We missed you at

dinner,' Phemie said lightly accusing but with a broad smile.

'I have to earn to keep all this afloat, Mrs Waugh. You know that.' David smiled, too, but Rosalie wasn't sure it reached his eyes.

'You mean Agnes isn't charging enough?'

'I couldn't possibly suggest such a thing to one of her guests, now could I?' David turned away then to look at the pipe Phemie had complained of. 'I saw Rosalie giving you a bit of a push over that pipe, Mrs Waugh. Has it always caused you a problem?'

'Oh, no. The last couple of visits, maybe. Do you think it's rising?'

'Maybe,' David answered, 'Or maybe the ground around it is sinking. Either way, I'll get someone to have a look. Are you going into the garden?'

'I need to get back to the kitchen,' Rosalie said, choosing a moment to get back to work. Although she was enjoying the older woman's company, she was conscious that while David and Mrs

Waugh knew each other, she was really the hired help. And the hired help ought not to be swanning about mid-morning.

'Must you, my dear? I suspect Grant and Alastair Craig will keep things going longer than they put on the agenda.' Phemie said. 'Why don't we all go and sit in the glazed terrace?'

'Sounds like a plan,' David said. 'Don't worry about your soup, Rosalie, I saw Mum in the kitchen as I came round. She knows a lot about soup.'

'I'm sure she does. The cock-a-leekie she served up on Monday was amazing, but she didn't hire me to . . . '

'Chat up the customers?' Phemie interrupted. 'When you're running a small enterprise like this one, that's definitely part of the brief.'

Rosalie glanced at David. He was busy taking the handles at the back of the wheelchair, but he smiled at her and nodded towards a low gate set into the hedge that surrounded the lawns in front of the house. She smiled back. Agnes was seeing to the soup and twenty minutes wasn't going to derail the serving of a cold buffet, she thought. Besides, her mother would be agog to hear about this glazed terrace so that would be something other than Steve Baxter to talk about the next time she phoned.

6

The rest of the Waughs visit passed off without problem and Rosalie started a notebook recording what had gone well and what not so well. She also noted down the menus she'd used because the Waughs might come again while she was employed here, and it would be good to know what she'd already fed them.

She was busy in the kitchen when Betty came in. She sent her a warm smile.

'Morning, Rosalie. The eggs,' Betty said and set a large box full of egg trays onto a counter. 'Bob brought them in because the suppliers are still trying to sort out a new driver.'

'Oh, what happened to the last one then?' Rosalie asked.

'She's on maternity leave. Baby's due week after next,' Betty said and came across to look over Rosalie's shoulder. 'That looks amazing. Are they the canapés for the wedding?'

Rosalie scooped the last sliver of beet-root mix onto a teaspoon and added it to the blobs already on the baking trays. 'Yep, that's the first batch. I'll need to rein myself in, though, because I've never catered for a wedding of nine guests before.'

'No, I don't suppose many chefs have. We usually have a marquee on the side-lawn for a hundred and fifty with all the rooms booked and teenagers bunking in the fishing cabins.' Betty sighed. 'Nine makes a pleasant change.'

'All that bed-linen,' Rosalie said sym-pathetically. 'Has everyone from the Waugh group gone?'

'Yes, they have,' Agnes said as she came into the kitchen. Rosalie was sur-prised by her grumpy tone. 'I've just had an unwelcome text from David.' She set her mobile on the edge of a counter and sank into a chair.

'Agnes, what's wrong? Has he had an accident?' Rosalie scanned Agnes's drawn features with dismay.

'An accident? No. He's arranged a viewing.'

'Oh,' Betty said, and nodding to Rosalie, began to walk towards the back stairs.

'Don't rush away, Betty. We're all in this,' Agnes said with an edge of sharpness Rosalie hadn't heard before. Betty leant against the door frame and let her handbag slide to the floor.

'I suppose there's no guarantee any buyer would keep on the present staff,' Betty said, and Rosalie realised that for Betty, that might mean her house as well because she and Bob lived in a cottage tied to his job as head gardener.

'So you mean a viewing as in people who want to buy the house, rather than come as guests?' Rosalie asked.

'I do. Has he mentioned to you how keen he is to sell-up?' Agnes directed a razor-sharp blue gaze towards her, and Rosalie blenched.

'Not in so many words, no,' she replied. 'He did warn me the first morning, while he was driving me here from the village, that he was the owner and you were his tenant.' Rosalie remembered David's words and how they'd made her feel very much on sufferance.

'Typical. Undermining your intention to stay before you even got started,' Agnes said crossly.

'Not exactly,' Rosalie said, 'I am looking for my next job, though, because you did take me on only for seven months.'

'That was just a formality, Rosalie. You know the sort of thing, in case you hated being in the country or you weren't prepared to co-operate with regulars like the Waughs who have their favourite foods. I was fairly sure I'd be happy with you, if you were happy with me.' Agnes caught hold of her mobile and slid it back and forth on the counter.

Rosalie felt a surge of compassion for this elderly lady whose business was under threat and wondered what they could do to put off prospective buyers. Given that the house and grounds were kept in such good order by Agnes and her staff, it was a hard task. She glanced around the kitchen and caught sight of some sawdust where Betty had set the egg box. No doubt the box had been on the floor of one of Bob's vans, she thought.

A flash of inspiration made her a little dizzy. She could work out where the sawdust came from. What if there were a little more and spread out in an attic or two?

'Does Bob have any sawdust going spare?' she asked Betty.

'I suppose,' Betty said with a quizzical glance. 'What would we be doing with that, then?'

'Oh, I don't know,' Rosalie mused. 'If I were exploring the attics and I happened to be carrying a bag of sawdust that had a tear in it . . .'

Agnes lifted her head from the careful study of her mobile and Rosalie saw the tiny gleam of hope light her eyes.

'It's also the case that the tap in the cloakroom on the mezzanine floor doesn't turn off too easily. What if we dyed the sink with some tea?' Rosalie added, warming to the theme.

'They'll get surveyors in, Rosalie. These ploys aren't going to fool a professional,' Agnes said with a resigned sigh.

'Maybe not, no, but they might buy us some time while the prospective buyers hesitate,' Rosalie said.

Agnes looked at her speculatively. 'Time,' she said.

'Yes,' Rosalie said firmly, 'And in that time, perhaps we could arrange for someone to lodge a planning application for something deeply unattractive to a prospective mansion-house owner.'

'Like an abattoir,' Betty said with a short laugh. 'Remember when the farmer down in Maldingtonon-Ure tried to get one approved.

'Oh, Betty, I think you're on to something there,' Agnes said. 'I remember the arguments well. I wonder if Tam Anscomb would consider applying to build a recycling treatment plant with capacity for two hundred lorries a day?'

'Why would he agree to that?' Rosalie asked. 'I thought he and David got on well.'

'Oh they do, Rosalie, but two things, my dear. Firstly, Tam and Sadie make a lot of incidental sales to the guests who stay here. If the business closes, they may find their shop unviable. Secondly, although Tam owns a field on the borders of the Maldington House estate. He doesn't actually have to lodge the application.'

'Of course not,' Rosalie agreed, beginning to see how Agnes's mind was working. 'He only has to be briefed and prepared to answer questions to give the impression he's going to do it.'

'I think I'll go into Wolcester and consult the local plan in the library,' Agnes said. 'No point in suggesting something that wouldn't even get past that first hurdle. Does a recycling plant or an abattoir count as light industry? I'm sure we must have some zoning for light industry as we're not actually in the national park.'

'Oh my!' Betty said feelingly as she lifted her bag and sent Rosalie a look filled with heartrending hope. 'Planning applications. I'm so glad you took the chance on coming here, Rosalie.'

Rosalie took a deep breath. This wasn't the moment to share her most recent history with Agnes and Betty, but she wished she could. As she slotted the canapés into the oven, she knew a tiny niggle of doubt and guilt. David Logie wasn't a bad man and his mother wasn't a young woman. On the other hand, she needed to keep this job going while she sorted out her finances and if there was a way to frustrate the house sale meantime, then she was in.

★ ★ ★

Rosalie parked the elderly Skoda Agnes made available for her to drive around the area under the sycamore in the village's main street the following morning. She just resisted the temptation of patting the little car on the bonnet. It was basic and had a dent in the rear that made the boot a bit difficult to close, but it was easy to drive and she wasn't exposed to the elements as she had been while job hunting in Newcastle on her dad's old bike.

The shop was open and she headed

there first. With a little of the cash from David Logie's advance on her wages, she'd decided to accept Tam and Sadie Anscomb's offer of a seat in their minibus and a ticket for the community drama. She knew she had to start finding her way back into some more normal activities than she'd been able to pursue since her business collapsed.

'Ah, it's Miss Garden,' Tam said as she entered the shop, 'I wondered who was brave enough to bring that old banger onto a public road. We could hear it before we saw it.'

'Bob assured me it had a valid MOT when he gave me the key,' Rosalie protested. 'Besides, it drives easily. I'm not worried about the appearance.'

'Quite right, Miss Garden. You can't see what it looks like when you're inside it driving.' Sadie spoke from the top of some steps and Rosalie had to crane her neck to return the warm smile sent her way.

'I heard from David Logie that you've reserved a ticket and a seat in the minibus for me for next week,' Rosalie said.

She unhitched her shoulder bag and drew out her purse.

'Now you put that away, Pet,' Tam said, and Sadie agreed as she came down the steps.

'Our treat to welcome you to the village, Lass. You'll be doing me a favour in fact, because Tam is always asleep before the villain appears,' Sadie said.

'It has a villain?'

'Aye, it's a spin-off Agatha Christie script, but while I dispute the allegation that I am asleep before the villain appears, I do find the seats in the little theatre rare and comfy.' Tam said frowning at his wife.

'Do they always do cosy crime, then?'

'Mostly. It's what the punters like, but you'll get a panto at Christmas.' The landline rang as Tam was speaking and he headed into the back-shop to answer it.

'I hope you'll still be around at Christmas, Miss Garden . . . '

'Please, call me Rosalie.'

Sadie nodded her agreement and

smiled. 'I do hope you'll like it here. We enjoy having the guests come in and out and Agnes's business does give a lift to the local economy.'

'I gather Dougie, my predecessor, was here for a longish stint. So maybe I'll enjoy the post, too.' Rosalie was looking through the rack of magazines when Tam came back into the front-shop. She lifted one of her favourites and thought she might treat herself as she wasn't going to have to pay for the theatre ticket. She wasn't really listening as Tam told his wife about the telephone call, but suddenly his words drew her in.

'A bloke up from Newcastle, apparently. Steve Baker or Baxter, something like that.'

'It could be Baxter, right enough,' Sadie agreed, 'Rick Easton has cousins called Baxter. He might have recommended him.'

Rosalie steadied herself by grabbing hold of the shop counter.

'Here, Miss Garden,' Tam said in worried tones, 'You've lost all your colour and us wittering on about egg delivery men. Here,' he came out from behind the counter dragging a chair, 'Sit thee down, Lass. Sit thee down.'

Rosalie sank onto the chair and took several deep breaths. Steve was a very common first name, she reminded herself silently. Also, she'd never heard her ex talk about relatives in this part of the country. It could not be him. Surely fate wouldn't be so unkind?

Even as the thoughts were churning in her head, Rosalie knew with a falling heart that it very well could be Steve. Her new life had been free of poison for less than a week.

7

Rosalie collected the final plates and missing bits of cutlery from the Peacock Room while Marcus and Mandy were taking coffee and liqueurs into the library where the wedding guests had withdrawn after their meal. She'd just set the final bowl onto a trolley when David spoke from the doorway.

'How did it go?' he asked amiably, and Rosalie felt a twinge of guilt. For all his threats to thrash out the failings that had brought down her business, he was always considerate when she was working on something here. It seemed underhand to be plotting with Agnes to put off his prospective house buyers.

'Hello, David. It went well, I think. No leftovers from the table and that's a good sign,' she said. 'Although I sometimes wonder if the ladies have been slimming for so long to get into their dress 'on the day', that they just let go and . . . '

'Pig out,' David finished for her. He laughed and the sound cheered her. It had been a worrying couple of days mulling over the prospect of Steve being in the area and she hadn't done a lot of smiling. 'It would certainly be tempting to pig out on your lovely food,' David added.

'Are you looking for Agnes?' Rosalie found it hard to hear compliments since the collapse of Dinners At Your Leisure and always tried to deflect them. Despite a full order book with waiting lists for some busy times of the year, being a good cook hadn't saved her business.

'I was. I sent her a text and she said she'd be around the kitchen area, but I didn't see her, so I came to check through here.' David glanced along the corridor from the open doorway but turned back almost immediately. 'She may have gone upstairs to her flat. Will you still be in the kitchen in twenty minutes?'

'I expect so. Marcus and Mandy will be heading off by then. They're serving coffee.' Rosalie wheeled the trolley out and across the carpeted hall to the service lift. It was only big enough to take the trolley and Rosalie watched its doors slide together. She hesitated before turning to go down the steps from the main floor to her domain in the kitchen because David was standing very close behind her and a smell touched her senses: whisky. He stepped back as though he suddenly realised he'd been crowding her.

'Sorry, not entirely with it. I had a glass or two with some friends in the pub and walked back with the dogs. I'll need to collect the car in the morning,' he said.

'It is Saturday,' Rosalie said.

'Saturday, yes, it is,' David murmured, and Rosalie glanced at his face. What she saw there made her determine to be out of the kitchen and shut in her rooms by the time he was free of his mother. Too much whisky might make David Logie think it'd be a good idea to get to know the staff better, but the morning would bring a different and sobering perspective on that, she thought.

Once in the kitchen, she whizzed

through the remaining chores. Just as she was crossing to the little stairway that led up to her rooms, she heard movement behind her.

A cool breeze tickled the back of her neck where she'd opened her tunic and she realised the outer door was open. Drat, she thought, one of the twins has left something. Turning around, she froze.

'Hullo, Rosalie,' Steve Baxter said from the kitchen doorway.

Stunned by his unexpected, unwanted presence, Rosalie could not speak. She curled her fingers into fists and jammed them into the pockets of her kitchen trousers.

'Unlike you to be tongue-tied, lover,' Steve said, and Rosalie flinched at the contempt in his tone. But it was that unwarranted contempt from a man who had taken everything from her except her professional knives, that broke her silence.

'This is private property. You are not welcome here,' she said finding her voice at last.

'I can only agree with Miss Garden,' David said from the other side of the kitchen. Rosalie hadn't heard him come in. 'This is private property and I must ask you to leave.'

The change in Steve's demeanour could hardly have been bettered by the Doigs at their acting school finest. Rosalie might have been taken in herself had she not experienced it so many times before.

'I am sorry,' Steve said without any trace of the contempt he'd used earlier, 'I'll be starting a delivery job around here on Monday and I borrowed a bike from my cousin, Rick Easton, to suss out the routes. When I saw the kitchen lights on, I thought I might introduce myself to the people. Didn't imagine I'd find the chef, though.'

'Delivery?' David asked and Rosalie thought he sounded a little suspicious.

'Yes, from LayBright Eggs. Rick put in a word for me. He farms locally, but I expect you know that. I'm recovering from a chronic illness, you see. The medics thought getting out of Newcastle and away from the hurly burly would be a good idea.'

Rosalie raised her eyes skywards.

David glanced from the intruder to his chef and shrugged. 'That's all very well, but it's more conventional to do these things in daylight and not scare the wits out of staff by turning up in the dark.' He took a couple of steps towards Steve who backed up.

'Rosalie and I are well known to each other,' Steve said holding his ground again. 'In fact, we were very well known to each other before . . . ' He let his words tail off into what a casual listener might think was regretful silence.

'Before?' David asked and Rosalie thought that sounded threatening.

Steve gave an apologetic cough. 'In New castle when Rosalie was self-employed. Of course, you may not understand everything, but I did my best to help when the business model she was pursuing turned out to be imploding.'

'Get out,' Rosalie shouted at him. 'Get

out and don't come back.'

'Well, as to that, Rosalie, I'm employed to deliver your egg order. I will be back.'

'Leave them in the courtyard, for crying out loud. Can't you understand I don't want to be in the same room as you, ever.' Rosalie turned on her heel and sped upstairs. Locking the door of her flat, she slid down it till she was crouching on the floor.

* * *

The tapping on her door was light, but persistent and Rosalie knew she'd have to answer. How could she face David Logie with tears streaming down her cheeks and her hair in a tumbling mess of pins and net?

'He's gone, Rosalie, and I've turned the key in the kitchen door. He won't be surprising you again,' David said. 'Please, just let me see you're okay and then I'll go, too, and leave you in peace.'

Rosalie shoved down on her heels and hauled herself into a standing position.

She screwed her hands into her eyes and, thinking better of that, grabbed a towel from the end of the bed to wipe her face. She took a deep gulp of air before unlocking the door to let David into her small bedsitting-room.

His tall frame loomed in the darkness and she heard him fumble behind his back until he found the wall switch. She sank onto the bed blinking in the light that flooded the room.

'We can keep the doors locked meantime,' David said, 'If you feel under any threat from that man.'

'You would recognise him,' Rosalie said. 'From the photo I dropped.'

'Yes, I did, although he's a bit more gaunt than when the photo was taken. He said he'd been ill?'

'Ill!' Rosalie twisted the towel in her hands. 'You could say.'

'But?' David wasn't backing off and she knew it was the moment when some at least of her past had to be shared.

'He's not ill, David. He's an alcoholic. When he says 'medics', he really means 'case worker'.' Rosalie sat up straighter and allowed David to unwind the towelling she'd wrapped around her hands. 'And when he says he tried to help save the business, he means he tried to carry on covering up how much he'd taken out of it.' Rosalie felt the strength of David's arms as he pulled her gently onto her feet. She was conscious of the rise and fall of his chest as he drew her into his body.

It would be so easy to fall for this man and let his strength be hers, but she knew she couldn't do that again. Surely Steve's effect on her tonight was evidence of what a mistake it was to rely so completely on someone else's strength?

'You're shivering,' he said. 'He has gone. I heard the dogs barking as his bike crunched over the gravel in the back drive.' Rosalie felt warmth grow in her as David's hand rubbed up and down her back, soothing as one would a fractious child or agitated grandparent. 'Rosalie.'

She snapped her head up and brought both her hands onto David's front. This couldn't happen. He was her boss. She squeezed out of his hold and he stood away.

'Sorry, sorry.'

'Me, too, David. I'm tired. It's been a long day and I have to serve breakfast at nine o'clock,' she said and knew the words weren't very far off being garbled. David stepped away and out onto the tiny landing.

'I would say we could get the eggs from elsewhere, but it would lead to all sorts of questions and speculation. You may feel it's easier to allow him to deliver them now you know to expect him,' David said.

'Of course, and it is only once a week,' Rosalie agreed, although she knew she'd be in a state of tension waiting for him to turn up. Besides, if leopards didn't change their spots, then she was confident Steve would act as he had always done. He'd maximise her discomfiture by changing his route and turning up on different days. What was he doing here anyway, she wondered. One thing she was sure of and that was that it had nothing to do with his health and everything to do with causing mischief.

'Ask Keith to sign off on deliveries for the next month,' David said as he reached for the banister at the top of the stairs. 'He's a pleasant chap, but he can be assertive when it's needed.'

8

Rosalie heard Agnes calling her name as she came into the kitchen from the cellar. Her employer was fully dressed and Rosalie blinked in surprise but then remembered Agnes had agreed to help serve breakfast as the Doigs were now officially off for the whole week.

'Ah, Rosalie, there you are. Our bride, Deirdre, would like everyone to have Buck's Fizz on the terrace,' Agnes said in slightly worried tones. 'Do we have enough fresh orange to serve them all?'

'I can manage that, Agnes,' Rosalie replied. 'Are they all gathered?' She knew breakfast was to be served promptly because the newly-weds were booked on a flight out of Newcastle airport at 12.30, but it might take a while to get everyone up. After the whole party was collected, it didn't seem long before Agnes was presenting the bill.

'That went really well, my dear. I

can't thank you enough,' Agnes said as she sat down at the kitchen table with a mug of hot chocolate. Rosalie heard the small thud as first one shoe and then the second was eased off and hit the floor. 'Deirdre's father has taken a wad of our business cards away with him to distribute at his golf club. He said there were several young who would be getting married, too, quite soon.'

'Wonder how he knows that?' David asked prosaically. He shut the kitchen door behind him and swiped the bolt across. Rosalie dipped her head over the dishwasher she was stacking. At least this morning, she was properly dressed and her hair was tidily secured.

'Who are we locking out?' Agnes asked.

'We had an unexpected visitor last night, after you went up. I agreed with Rosalie that we would keep the door secured for a couple of days anyway.' David didn't mention who the visitor had been, and Rosalie was grateful to him for the interval to gather her wits. However, she knew Agnes would need to be told and surely it was better to offer the information than have it drawn out of her.

'The visitor was Steve Baxter, my ex-fiancé,' she said.

'Oh,' Agnes's dismay would have been comical in other circumstances, but Rosalie was too nervy to appreciate it fully. 'Does he want you to go back to Newcastle?'

'What?' Rosalie was astonished by the question. 'No, of course not. It truly is over between us.' She shut the dishwasher with such force the china rattled. 'He told us he's come to work here and is the replacement for the LayBright eggs' driver.'

'Patty Ingram,' Agnes said and took another sip of her chocolate.

'Yes, Patty's baby is due rather soon,' David said, 'I don't know how she was carrying laden egg boxes around.'

'As to that, a girl like Patty never did much of the actual carrying,' Agnes said dryly. 'I don't suppose we'll see your young man this week, though, Rosalie, because we've an empty diary and don't need any eggs.'

Rosalie dropped her gaze. How hard was it going to be to make Agnes and the others believe Steve hadn't followed her here with hope in his heart? Even David looked less certain this morning. When his mother referred to Steve as 'your young man', he'd lifted a gaze to her face which she knew was flushed. She also knew it was flushed through irritation and not the romantic embarrassment the others were looking for.

'Mother, give Rosalie a break, why don't you. She's already said it's over between her and this man. If I could change the subject,' David said as the kitchen door rattled in its frame behind him. He turned round and slid back the bolt. 'Good morning, Betty. Sorry about that.'

'Morning, everyone,' Betty said. She was clearly bewildered to find the door locked but didn't ask why directly. 'All right?'

'Apparently David and Rosalie had

an unwanted intruder last night,' Agnes said to her housekeeper.

'Really?' Betty was surprised. 'A burglar?'

'No,' Agnes said, 'The new egg delivery man.'

'Goodness gracious,' Betty said, 'That's keen. Bob met him in the shop earlier. Says he's a cousin of Rick and Hazel at Highcroft. Anyways, I'll be getting on.'

They watched Betty slip away to change shoes and begin the job of stripping beds and cleaning en-suites. Once she'd pulled the door closed behind her David turned to his mother again.

'Yes, there's nothing in the diary for this coming week and I've booked in two lots of people to view the house.'

'Two,' Agnes protested, 'You said one, last week.'

'Word is getting out, Mum.' David said and Rosalie heard Agnes's intake of breath.

'I'm sure it is. You've been assiduous in placing adverts,' Agnes retorted.

'Clearly you don't get your admin genes from me.'

'Mum! What is the point of having something to sell and not bringing it properly into the market? Of course I've advertised.'

Rosalie wondered why she hadn't seen any of the sale particulars when she applied for the job of chef and thought perhaps she'd contented herself with a quick Google to see what the house looked like; and a check of the advertising for the guest house business.

Once she'd established that the business was real, and indeed thriving, she'd concentrated on getting herself here. Would she have accepted the job if she'd known about this family dispute, she wondered.

Agnes set her mug down with a decidedly bad-tempered snap. Chocolate splashed up and dribbled down the outside. She pulled an embroidered hanky from her sleeve and mopped up the drips.

'Mum,' David said, 'There's really no need for all this drama. It'll take some months for the business to go through, even if we find a suitable buyer quickly, and I have promised that the grounds will be divided in such a way that you'll be able to carry on with your exhibition garden.'

'Yes, from a small flat over a shop in Wolcester.'

'It'll be the house we've identified on the High Street and you're living in a small flat over the shop here, aren't you?'

Agnes stood up and drew back her shoulders. 'That was a low blow.' She left the kitchen in her stockinged feet.

Rosalie sent David a reproachful look. It wasn't anything to do with her, of course, but she was becoming fond of her employer. At the same time, she could only imagine how many similar arguments had taken place since David had decided to split the estate and sell the big house.

'Do not judge me, Rosalie Garden.'

Heat flamed over Rosalie's neck and face. He was right. She had no idea of the pain he must suffer when he thought about what might have been. If he and Libby had had any hope of children, then it must be hard to drive past the house knowing that would never happen.

'I beg your pardon,' she said. 'It must be really difficult to keep the house on when you may have no intention of living in it again. I suppose now you've decided to sell you'll want to get it underway.'

David sighed heavily. 'Don't be so damned reasonable, woman.'

'What!'

'Reasonable. Why aren't you siding with Mum in order to keep your job going? Maybe the appearance of Baxter has caused second thoughts.' He crossed the kitchen and bent down to retrieve Agnes's shoes from under the table. Straightening up, he fixed his intelligent gaze on her and Rosalie narrowed her eyes.

'Steve's presence in the area is unwanted but it won't make me abandon my contract,' she said.

'Good. The first lot of prospective buyers are coming tomorrow morning at 11am. Obviously, I'll be here to show them around.' Rosalie watched him take the shoes into the corridor.

She lifted the abandoned mug and added it to the dish-washer load. Betty came through with a bag of accumulated rubbish to take out to the dustbins, but she had to put it down in order to unbolt the door.

'Let's forget about that for now, Betty. It's clearly a nuisance.' Rosalie lifted the rubbish and handed it to the house-keeper. She didn't know what was going on in Steve's head, but she would obviously keep her own little flat locked up while he remained in the district.

'Thanks, Rosalie. It does make it a bit inconvenient having to down everything to get out and then knock to get back in,' Betty said before disappearing into the yard.

David came back. 'Would this be a good time to have our interview?' he asked.

Rosalie bit back the instinct to say there was no good time and nodded.

'If you wouldn't mind coming across to the carriage house, please, it'll give us a bit of privacy we won't achieve here.' David had hardly finished when they heard a car draw into the back courtyard. David glanced out.

'Mum's sister, Alice. She'll go in through the conservatory.' David held the kitchen door open for her and they left the warm haven of Rosalie's domain.

* * *

Rosalie should have asked David for ten minutes grace to change out of her kitchen whites, she thought, as they entered Carriage House. She felt at a major disadvantage in her uniform. In the beautiful surroundings of his unique home, she stood out as the employee.

'I'll get the coffee,' David said. 'Clashes with Mum take it out of me.' There was a tiredness and a sadness behind his words that Rosalie picked up on.

'Thank you, I'd love some,' she said. The room they entered was open plan with a fitted kitchen close to the outer door and a comfortable sitting area further into the building. They were separated by an antique oak table and chairs. Rosalie ran her hand over the surface.

'Probably covered in dust,' David turned back from the kettle carrying two steaming mugs. He nodded towards a fridge. 'Milk if you'd like.'

Rosalie took a carton of semi-skimmed from the fridge door and followed David through the ground-floor to an office at the rear. It had a business end and a studio with his huge architectural easel under a glass roof. The studio was thrust out through a cut-away in the wall and sloping roof of the original carriage house.

'This is lovely,' she said.

'Yes,' David agreed. 'We were happy with it and I can keep the extra bedrooms closed up now I'm on my own.' He set the mugs down and gestured to a comfortable small armchair.

Sitting down, Rosalie silently absorbed that unself-conscious 'we'. Libby was clearly still a very big part of his thinking. She gazed round the room at the mounted drawings and photographs of David's projects so far. Despite being only thirtyish, there were a fair number and they were mostly one-off houses in rural areas.

★ ★ ★

David lifted his coffee as he sat down opposite Rosalie and put it on a small table at his elbow. He was determined not to lose control of this interview in the way he felt things had got out of hand when he gave Rosalie her salary advance. He was deeply aware of how relaxed she'd become with his mother. She certainly wasn't relaxed now, and he knew any progress they'd made had been set right back by Steve Baxter's appearance last night.

'I don't think this will take us very long, Rosalie,' he said. 'I did look up your business, Dinners At Your Leisure online as I told you the other night.'

'Yes, I think the domain name runs out the week after next,' she said, and he sensed the exasperation. Was she thinking that if he'd waited, he wouldn't have found out how well it was doing? Or was she regretful that her hard won reputation would disappear with the website?

'Did you hope to have the business back in action before then?'

'No, not at all. The debt was too deep for any kind of resurrection.' Rosalie swirled the coffee around in her mug but didn't meet his gaze.

'I'm really sorry. Being self-employed, I do understand the fine line we all tread between feast and famine and . . . ' He caught the flash of irritation in her eyes before she dropped her gaze back to the coffee. 'Sorry, a badly chosen comparison.'

'Look, Mr Logie, what is it you need to know? I don't have any criminal history — check it out. I made a few bad, very bad business mistakes, but with my father's help, I've repaid all the creditors.' She swallowed hard, and David did hope they weren't going to have tears. 'All of them.'

'I'm really glad because that will help you as you return to the business world. What worries me, though, is what those wrong decisions were. You seem to me to be a hard-working person with determination and a clear head.' David swallowed some of his own drink. The bitter black liquid helped him focus. 'And also, what part in all of this does Steve Baxter play? Why is he here?'

'I have no idea why he's here,' Rosalie replied forcefully, and David realised he'd given her an out by asking two questions at once. He did need the answer to them both. She lifted those wonderful eyes now shimmering with anger and staring directly at him. 'He is not here at my instigation.'

'I thought not, but he has gone to a lot of effort to come into the area, hasn't he? Swapping work as an accountant to drive an egg delivery round.' David thought about that and realised Steve was probably living on the farm with his

cousin. 'And live in one of Rick's bothies.'

'Steve Baxter's comfort is no concern
of mine, Mr Logie. None at all. He's
been pestering my mother to get my
whereabouts. I expect she let something
slip.' Rosalie sighed and David thought
it sounded genuinely regretful.

'Well, let's leave that to one side, shall
we? Can you help me understand how a
business with a full order book and waiting lists went under so quickly?'

Later, David realised he'd lost her at
the mention of Rick's bothy. He'd seen
her fingers tighten on the mug handle so
hard they turned white. Did she think he
was ganging up in a blokes together sort
of way, he wondered. Whatever tipped
the scales, she withdrew any pretence of
cooperating with him.

'Clearly, as Steve said, the business
model I was using didn't cover all the
bases. I should perhaps have had more
outside advice.' She sent him a challenging glare and he felt his toes curl. Libby
had been inclined to do just that when

she thought he was asking questions about her care she couldn't, or wouldn't, answer.

'It's all very well to adopt an attitude, Rosalie, but it doesn't really help. Don't you want to move on from here into another upmarket position? Executive chef, at least?' He held her glance until she dropped it and set her cup onto the table. Every sinew in her neck and face was tight. 'My mother always let Dougie run his own books, ordering food, and wine where the guests don't bring their own. Should I be taking that on?'

'Provisioning the kitchen in case I run off with the budget? Really, Mr Logie . . .'

'Don't call me that,' David snapped, and faced up to the fact he'd lost control of the interview again. Libby always teased him by calling him Mr Logie. Everyone who'd known them had heard and now avoided it. Except Tam, but then he used the formal mode of address for all and sundry. Hearing the words still affected David. He stood up and walked across to the glass wall of the studio and gazed out into the policies of his inheritance. How long, he wondered, did a person, a sane person, go on grieving?

When he turned back to the room, Rosalie had gone. A whiff of scent hung in the air. Was it hers? Was he remembering Libby's?

9

Rosalie wondered if you could be fired for walking out on an interview with your employer's son, but decided she no longer cared. She'd landed this job and there were no doubt others. Perhaps it was time to listen to her dad's pleas to stop worrying about the money she owed him and get out of here. The atmosphere wasn't exactly toxic, but what with David Logie in a strop, Agnes in the huff and Steve in the district, she'd been in better places.

'Rosalie,' Agnes said as she crossed the yard outside the kitchen, 'I've just waved my sister Alice off. We came to find you so I could introduce her, but you weren't in the kitchen.'

'Sorry,' Rosalie said automatically, 'I went over to Carriage House with Mr Logie. He's been keen to understand why my own business had to be wound up.'

'Fretting over what doesn't concern him, I suspect,' Agnes said and led the way back into the big house. 'Don't let him bully you, my dear, this business belongs to me.'

'Well, yes, but he owns your premises.' Rosalie breathed in the smell of her domain: orangey this morning. The dishwasher was thrumming efficiently and somewhere else in the house a hoover was buzzing.

She saw the marmalade pulp she'd taken out of a freezer earlier on with a view to making it into the preserve for breakfasts. Did she want to give this up so quickly and what about the money she owed her parents? Despite her dad's reassurances, she knew they needed it back. She raised a hand to cover the sob that rose in her throat. 'Rosalie! My dear, what did that son of mine say to upset you?'

'Nothing I haven't thought of before, Agnes, honestly. Sometimes, though, it can all be a little overwhelming.'

Agnes didn't look much reassured, so

107

Rosalie made a huge effort to calm down and get on with some normal, mundane tasks: like making marmalade. She lifted a preserving pan out of the pots' store and set it onto the hob.

'Leave that for a moment, why don't you? I've been checking up on some of our counter-the-sale proposals,' Agnes said and closed the kitchen door. 'Alice's husband was a planning officer and she's found out one or two things for us.'

'Such as?' Rosalie asked. Agnes was clearly more cheerful than she had been earlier. 'Could Tam Anscomb lodge an appeal for a re-cycling plant?'

'He could and I'm just going to pop down to the village to tell him where to get the right forms and such like.'

Rosalie raised an eyebrow. Her employer seemed very sure that Tam would play along with this ploy.

Agnes picked up on her reaction. 'Don't worry, I'll make sure to ask him, not tell him and, of course, I'll get Sadie onside, too.' Agnes put the kettle on. 'Coffee?'

'No, I had coffee with Mr . . . with David,' she corrected herself, 'Thanks.' She poured her measured sugar slowly into the pan and stirred. 'Did Dougie make this pulp?'

'I think David did, actually,' Agnes replied, and Rosalie absorbed the information silently. 'He's a good cook of certain things. Not a good cook like you, of anything.'

'I'll have to be sure to leave a jar or two for him tomorrow morning. The first viewers are coming at 11 o'clock.'

'Are they, indeed. You'd better get up into the attics with that bag of sawdust, then. Bob was out at the foot of the kitchen garden and I popped into the woodshed while he was down there.'

Rosalie was momentarily puzzled by the reference to sawdust and then remembered she'd suggested laying a trail so people might think there was an insect infestation.

She concentrated hard on whether she could hear any sugar left undissolved in her pan. Deciding it was all right, she turned the heat up.

'Sawdust?' she asked and looked round. There was a scrappy carrier bag leaning drunkenly against the door to the main house corridor. 'Is the attic stair off your landing?' Even if no one was fooled for any length of time, there would be a childish satisfaction in sticking a spoke in David Logie's plans.

'It is,' Agnes said with a nod. 'Why don't you go up now while Betty is hanging out sheets? What she doesn't see, she can't accidentally comment on. I'll keep an eye on the pan.'

'Good idea,' Rosalie agreed. 'The marmalade is at a rolling boil and I usually allow about forty minutes for it to reach setting point.'

'You'll be back in ten. It's a hint of a few unwanted beasties we're leaving, not a suggestion the roof is caving in,' Agnes said and laughed.

* * *

Rosalie checked her watch as she dropped back down the attic staircase to the landing outside Agnes's flat. Fifteen minutes had been enough time to leave a few piles of sawdust in accessible but not obvious places. Some of the joists showed evidence of where insect damage had been treated, probably many years ago, and she'd dropped a couple of handfuls at those sites. Now she was wondering what to do with the carrier bag and its remaining load.

A through draught from the downstairs' door lifted the hair around her ears and alerted her to a possible caller in the kitchen. Delivery man, she wondered, or had David come over to the main house.

Pushing further open the door that concealed Agnes's stair from visitors' attention, she heard voices in the kitchen. She could hardly wander back in there carrying a tatty plastic bag that was dripping sawdust and cobwebs in equal measures. She spotted the cloakroom across the corridor and opening its door surveyed the little room. There was a Victorian Hope chest with a basket of towels sitting on it. Quickly, Rosalie lifted the basket off and raised the chest lid. She dropped the bag in and reinstated everything. It would do meantime, but she would have to remember to retrieve the remaining sawdust later. Swiftly, she washed her hands and tucked her hair back into its pins as best she could, before dropping down to meet whoever was entertaining Agnes.

Her employer was laughing as Rosalie came into the kitchen, but she stood still in dismay.

'Hullo, Rosalie, Pet. I was just making myself known to Mrs Logie here because Rick tells me she's the boss and I needed to meet her.' Steve said and sent Agnes a beaming smile like the ones he'd always bestowed on her mother, and Rosalie noticed how it had exactly the same effect on this older lady.

Agnes was well on the way to being smitten by Steve's clever mix of deference and outrageousness. How, she would be thinking soon, could this delightful man be anything but misunderstood? Rosalie knew with heart-stopping anger that any criticism would be brushed aside as unjustified or, worse, spiteful.

'Good morning, Steve.' Rosalie skirted the central table and made for the pan of marmalade. She glanced at the kitchen clock. A few more minutes should bring the batch to its setting point.

She kept her back to the others as she worked, conscious of the tension building in the room. Agnes, whose impeccable manners encompassed even delivery drivers pushing their luck, and their presence, where it wasn't wanted, would be desperate for Rosalie to pay Steve some attention. Steve would be determined to provoke a reaction from her that allowed him to retreat in a wounded but unbowed manner.

Rosalie had had her share of Steve's power games and she had no intention of playing them here. If he intended to turn up unannounced then the kitchen door would have to be kept locked and

Betty would have to be inconvenienced.

As if she were on some sort of psychic link, Betty chose that moment to stagger in with a huge basket of laundry. Steve caught the basket as Betty tripped over his satchel and dropped it.

'Oh, look, I'm sorry, Pet. That's my satchel you've tripped over.' Rosalie turned in time to see Steve set the laundry onto the kitchen table and catch Betty by the arm. 'My fault, Miss. Sorry.'

'Betty,' Agnes asked, 'Are you all right, my dear?'

'I'm fine, Mrs Logie. Just need to catch my breath,' Betty said, and allowed Steve to ease her onto one of the upright chairs. 'I'm fine,' she repeated, as Steve would have apologised again, 'But if you've business in this kitchen on a regular basis, maybe you'd take better care of your belongings.'

Steve bowed his head in what Rosalie recognised as a parody of meekness, but the other ladies both had smiles playing around their mouths. Rosalie returned to her marmalade wondering whether it was cool enough to pot it up yet; because if not she would have to take herself out of the kitchen while Steve remained in it.

'If you're sure you're okay, I'd better get back on the road. My schedule isn't too tight today, but as it's my first day, I'd really like to complete it in good time.'

'Of course,' Agnes said with a laugh, 'I hope we haven't kept you too long, Steve. It was very considerate of you to drop by.'

And there we have it, Rosalie thought. Steve swans in where he has no legitimate business, nearly causes an accident and yet, and yet, Agnes is apologising for keeping him back.

And it worked on me, too, for three long years.

Keith Brodie came into the kitchen. He was a thick-set man of middle height with a lot of hair he kept tied back in a ponytail. Like many of the staff in the country, Rosalie was discovering, Keith had several ploys. Besides being Agnes's kitchen porter four days in the week, he worked behind the bar in a pub in

Wolcester and also helped his brother with a garage specialising in classic cars.

'Who is that bloke?' he asked without preamble, nodding backwards to the kitchen door.

'Good morning to you, too, Keith,' Agnes said repressively, but Keith wasn't repressed. 'I mean, when I was casting a line or two in the river last night, he came thundering down the path on an old bike muttering to himself.'

'Muttering?' Betty asked. 'Had you been at the left-over champers, then. Keith?'

'There were no leftover champers. Muttering, he was. Something about how some folk had landed on their feet whatever, but he'd landed in Rick's bothy.' Keith cast his eyes down. 'Sorry Mrs L.'

'And so you should be, Keith, that was Rosalie's fiancé,' Agnes said.

'Agnes, please, he is not in any kind of relationship with me,' Rosalie said.

Keith grinned. 'No way, Mrs L. Rosalie's only been here a few days, but you can tell she has better taste than that character. Look I'm not on here today. I just came in to collect my script for the play. Won't tell you what part I'm playing, but I can sell you a ticket.'

'We've got tickets,' Betty said and he headed out to the staff lockers. After a few minutes they heard his cheerful whistle crossing the yard.

Rosalie carried on with her marmalade project and refused to join in the chat between Agnes and Betty. Wyn, the other member of their housekeeping staff, came down from the bedrooms looking for her morning coffee and was regaled by the story of Betty's trip. By the time Betty and Wyn headed back upstairs to finish the rooms, Rosalie was at screaming point.

'Your shoulders are rigid,' Agnes said conversationally. 'I'm sorry things haven't worked out for you and that rather nice young man, but you'll know your own mind.'

'Oh, I do,' Rosalie said and immediately regretted it. Agnes had spent around twenty minutes with Steve. Hardly long enough to learn anything of substance about him. 'Sorry, that was rude. There is no hope of a reconciliation, Agnes, however.'

'Things have a way of working out. I really must get down to the village now,' Agnes said. She took the key of one of the estate cars from its hook and lifted her battered shoulder bag. Rosalie had noticed how out of sync it was with Agnes's usual smart appearance but didn't feel she'd been around long enough to ask about it.

'Would you cover the telephone for me while I'm out, please? Most bookings come by e-mail these days, but there is still the odd one from the landline.'

'I can do that. Good luck with your mission.'

Rosalie was sorting out the food left over from their weekend guests when the telephone rang and without a second thought, she picked up the receiver with one hand and reached over the counter to take a pen out of the jar of useful bits and pieces with the other.

'Good morning, Maldington House. How may I help?'

'That's a lot friendlier than you were in person,' Steve said in her ear. Rosalie held the receiver away and looked at it as if it might bite. Taking a breath or two to steady herself she brought it back. 'I asked what makes you think you can get away with all this superior holier than thou crap? It won't be like that once they know what a thief they have in their nest, will it?'

'What do you want, Steve?'

'What's mine. What you took from me against the promise of life-long companionship.' She heard him cough. He tried to keep speaking, but Rosalie realised he wasn't going to make it. The coughing gathered strength and eventually he hung up.

Rosalie replaced the phone and the pen. What was he ranting about, she wondered. Like others with the same sort of problems, Steve was much inclined to believe he was the wronged party. Had she still got anything of his? She'd even

119

had to sell her engagement ring. The mounting interest demands on her had become too much to resist. Surely Steve didn't think he had any entitlement to it? She'd only parted with it after she discovered the new Merc he'd bought was missing without trace. Without trace and, therefore, without any financial help that could be achieved by its sale.

10

On Tuesday morning Rosalie wandered through the kitchen garden following behind Bob. He'd already pointed out where she could cut flowers for the tables and the abandoned pigsty, when they stopped beneath an arch covered in a climbing rose.

'It's not edible, of course, but Mrs L is very keen on her roses. Not quite so keen as she is on the rhoddies. Have you been down the gorge to take a look? Still a fair few in bloom although the year is getting on?' Bob brought his monologue to a halt and Rosalie smiled up at the big man in his faded blue dungarees.

'They smell divine. Roses always make me feel a little drunk when I breathe in their perfume. The garden is in such good order, Bob.'

'Aye, weel. I've been here man and boy, Miss Rosalie. I dinna right know how I'll fill in my time if the new owners dinna want to keep me on,' he said, and Rosalie's heart skipped. She knew only too well how unnerving it was to be working up to and beyond capacity one day and sitting on your hands the next. If it hadn't been for the intervention of her father and a few remaining close friends, she wasn't sure how she would have got through the dark days after she was locked out of her business premises by the bailiffs.

There was nothing she could say that would help Bob so she contented herself by patting his arm sympathetically.

'Aye, weel,' Bob said again and then as if the tiny bit of physical contact had given him courage, he hurried on.

'You see, Miss Rosalie, there's a wee bitty of a problem where Betty is concerned.' He reached down and pulled a weed or two out of the earth around the rose. Clutching them in his hand, he started walking again.

Rosalie had come into the garden for a bit of a break from the inventory of stores she'd been making, and when Bob found her studying the fruit patch, he'd taken her on another tour to show her the parts she didn't get into first time round. She hadn't expected this heart to heart but didn't want to break the spell. Besides liking Bob hugely, she wondered if he might say something to help with their campaign to prevent the house sale.

'What is the problem with Betty?' Rosalie asked.

'She had a difficult time in school what with being from such a big family and a feckless dad. She didn't always get there and then she fell behind and . . . ' He stopped and stared into the middle distance. 'Well, to cut to the thing, Miss Rosalie, she can't read.'

Bob took out a huge red and white checked hanky and blew his nose. 'So, this job is near perfect for her because there's really no call to be reading and Mrs Logie is very understanding about her not picking up the telephone. She couldn't record any messages, you see.'

'That is a big problem,' Rosalie said and realised it was an understatement.

'I hadn't noticed but I'll take it into account. She does everything else well, though. She's been a great help to me trying to settle in.'

'She does do her stuff and all. However, she's another reason it would be good if Mr David doesn't manage to sell the house out from under his mother just at present. We've been thinking about a wee one. Then Betty could do part time, like. Especially when I could be keeping an eye on a pram or a toddler — like my dad did wi' me.'

'Yes, and she would have another family to think about rather than her unhappy memories,' Rosalie agreed. And, she wondered silently, would a baby's early books be a way for Betty to learn to read? She decided to find out when she had a spare moment.

Bob nodded. 'Thank you, Miss Rosalie, not everybody understands how folk can just fall through the system and find themselves too embarrassed to get it sorted.'

'They don't,' Rosalie said with a sigh,

'I'm only just thinking it through myself. Bob, Miss Rosalie is making me a bit nervous. Any chance it could be just Rosalie?'

Bob gave her a thumbs up and they parted company. Rosalie headed back into the house with a huge bundle of rhubarb and a smaller basket of early strawberries from the greenhouses.

* * *

David entered the kitchen more nervously than the day he'd gone into the headmaster's study after being reported for clambering among the school's many sloping roofs. On that teenage occasion, he'd had no hope of absolution and he still winced when he thought about the Head's withering scorn. How dare he endanger his life, the lives of others while the fire brigade attended to talk him down . . . On and on until his knees quaked.

He really hoped Rosalie would be in a more receptive frame of mind than old

Smythy had been all those years ago. Straightening his shoulders, he strode in and found the kitchen in its Marie Celeste mode. Files were strewn across the big central table and the chef's laptop was sitting open displaying a screen-saver. All that build up for nothing left him disorientated. He set his own folder of documents down.

David glanced at the kitchen clock. Ten-thirty. His first prospective buyers were arriving at eleven and neither the chef nor his mother were anywhere to be seen. He briefly toyed with the thought that the ladies were boycotting the visitors but gave himself a mental shake.

'Neither of them is a petulant child,' he said aloud and regretted it immediately as Rosalie spoke from behind him.

'Who do you encapsulate in that category, David?' she asked with a sweetness he recognised as sarcastic. 'I believe Agnes has gone down to the village to ask after a seat on tonight's minibus.'

'She has?' David was surprised. His

mother paid a certain amount of lip-service to the benefits of community drama, but really, she preferred to go down to Gateshead and take in a few nights at The Sage, from time to time. 'Music, classical music, is more her thing.'

'She mentioned that, but she also said she wanted to catch up with a few folk who'd be around in the interval.' Rosalie spoke without irony. David, however, had a good idea of the few folk his mother would be accosting at the production. What was she plotting, he wondered.

'Do you know if she intends to be here for the site visit?' He realised instantly that he'd chosen the wrong word. Site visit might be how he viewed it, but this was his mother's home and Rosalie's workplace. It wasn't tactful to imply the deal was done and dusted.

'I think she'll be here. What would you like the kitchen to provide?'

'Provide?' David was puzzled.

'Yes. Morning coffee? I've made a batch of scones.' He followed the sweep of Rosalie's arm to where something sat under a tea-towel. 'And there's some shortbread left from the wedding.'

He watched her cross the room to where the storage tins sat and saw the way her shoulders sagged when she lifted the end one and felt its weight. The content of the tins was available for anyone taking a break in the kitchen, so maybe one or two of the staff had helped themselves.

'Oh dear,' she said as she opened the lid and peered inside, 'Vultures are the Doig twins.'

'Maybe not just them. Betty and Wyn have been known to enjoy the odd bit of shortbread.' He laughed. 'Something you should be used to.'

'What?'

'Your cooking is so good, Rosalie, leftovers aren't really going to linger. The scones will be great. Thank you for thinking of them. I know you're probably on Mum's team where the plan to sell is concerned, but I appreciate it.'

David wondered why his words affected Rosalie so much. There was a tiny blush spreading up her neck and touching her cheeks. Surely she was used to compliments over her cooking? Whatever, he thought, the touch of vulnerability suited her better than the brittle shell they'd been getting used to.

'Look, about the other day. I'm sorry I snapped at you. The thing about my name is to do with Libby. She always called me Mr Logie. Even when we were teens at school. It was her way of pricking my pomposity, I suppose.' David shuffled the papers Rosalie had lying out and stopped as he realised she'd probably have them in a particular order.

'You were pompous?' Rosalie asked. 'You strike me as being quite, I don't know, egalitarian?'

'Teenage arrogance is something else. She was justified.'

'Right, well, I'm sorry too. It didn't occur to me.'

'No, why would it? You never met her or saw us together. It's my bad.'

'Curiously, I just asked Bob not to call me Miss Rosalie,' she said, and let her clear-eyed gaze slide away.

David had an unnerving sensation that Rosalie had been going to say something else then, but she turned her attentions to preparing a trolley of coffee and scones for the visitors. He watched her slender figure moving back and forward. Despite the moment of quiet, she didn't say anything else.

* * *

Rosalie was adding a jug of milk to the trolley before releasing it to Betty who was going to put it into the service lift, just as Agnes came in the back door from the village. The older woman looked a little flushed and Rosalie raised an eyebrow in enquiry, but Agnes shook her head.

'Later,' she said mysteriously. 'When the lottery winners have taken themselves off.'

'Are they really?' Betty asked. 'A big win?' Her eyes were stretched so wide, Rosalie almost laughed.

'Apparently,' Agnes said. 'Well, it

130

would need to be to contemplate taking Maldington on and reinstating it as a family home.'

'You'd need a big family, too, to do that,' Betty added, 'Otherwise you'd be rattling round in it. There are two people carriers out front.'

'Won't the lottery people send minders round with them?' Agnes gave a short laugh. 'To make sure people like David don't take advantage.'

Rosalie was a little startled by Agnes's antipathy, but decided not to encourage it. After all, David had inherited this large house and following the death of his wife, perhaps his plan was a good one. She knew she was conflicted by her own need to earn money, but he'd said it would take several months to sort out the handover and she'd surely, surely have found another job by then.

'I suppose I'd better go through. Are you pouring, Betty?'

'Can do Mrs L.'

Rosalie went back to the inventory of stores she'd been working on but had hardly made any progress when the house intercom buzzed.

'Rosalie, could you come into the Peacock Room, please? Mr and Mrs Mundell would like to meet you.' Although David's voice was calm Rosalie detected an air of mild panic in the request. She hadn't expected to be interviewed by the prospective buyers. Taking a quick glance in the mirror Agnes kept beside the hand sink, she tucked some hair into her French knot and smoothed her tee-shirt over her trousers. Should she put on her tunic, she puzzled, but decided against it. It was bound to be dusted with flour from her scone making and dripping that over the Peacock carpet wouldn't be the best plan.

* * *

The door to the Peacock Room was wide open and Rosalie could see three groups of people. David and Agnes stood together quite close to Betty and the trolley. Four people, in what might be described as a parody of country clothing, wandered around the room restlessly fingering the padding on the seats and running their hands over the polished wood of the table. To one side, three young people in country suits and carrying clipboards, alternately shuffled from foot to foot or moved purposefully towards the bay windows overlooking the side lawns and back again.

Rosalie realised immediately that all was not going as well as it might and also that they hadn't even been up into the attics so her activities with the bag of sawdust were as yet unknown. Mr Mundell Sr was a large and florid gentleman in his late sixties and he took it on himself to introduce the others cutting David off mid-sentence.

'David here said his mother had a chef,' he grumbled. 'No matter, we're into equality. Aren't we, Gert? This is my wife.' He waved a hand in the direction of a sulky looking woman around his own age. 'The kind of equality that says she owns a half of everything.' He winked, and Rosalie was momentarily dumbstruck. She wondered whether the real prospective buyers had been persuaded to allow friends of the Doigs to stand in for them.

The younger man stepped forward bringing the other woman with him. 'Hullo, Miss Garden. I'm Ted and this is my wife, Lauren. We'd be living here, too, if Dad and Mum go ahead and buy Maldington House.'

Rosalie shook hands with everyone and waited. She still couldn't work out why they'd wanted to meet her.

'Do you, like, come with the house?' Lauren asked.

'No, no,' she said in what she hoped was a neutral tone. 'You'll be able to do your own thing or employ your own chef. Are you hoping to do a lot of entertaining?'

'Entertaining?' the younger man asked, and Rosalie saw she'd chosen the wrong word.

'Sorry, I mean dinners and parties, that sort of thing.'

They all spoke at once.

'No', the girl said, breathing the word in panic.

'Aye, just the job. Let them jealous Bs from the bowls see what they're missing out on,' Mr Mundell said and punched his son playfully on the arm.

'Right on, Will. You at the head of that table. We'll be buying the furniture as well, won't we?' Gert asked.

'Mention of parties cheered you up, didn't it?' Will said and guffawed. Lauren slunk away to one side of the room and drew Ted with her. They began to whisper urgently.

'You must be wondering why Mr and Mrs Mundell asked to meet you, Miss Garden,' one of the accompanying minders said. 'They're struggling to understand the nature of Mrs Logie's business here and wondered if you could tell them a little about it. It might be something for them to keep up, now that they don't go out to work.'

'Oh,' Rosalie said, surprised, 'I only started work here recently.'

'Exactly, Lass,' Mr Mundell said, 'Not in with the bricks so you'll be seeing it with a fresh eye.'

Rosalie avoided looking at either David or Agnes. What must be going through their heads, she wondered. 'I see. Maldington is run as a country house guest house. So, people hire it for biggish gatherings when they want good food, country pursuits and privacy. The first event I catered was a corporate away one for a board of directors and their spouses. I've also done a very small wedding, but with the space for a marquee, there are likely to be bigger weddings over the summer.'

'So, that's all by arrangement?' Gert Mundell asked.

'Yes, nobody comes up the drive and books a room. It's different from a small hotel in that respect. Mrs Logie knows in advance who'll be coming.'

'Any big names in the diary, then?' she asked, and Rosalie began to understand where this was going. Mrs Mundell didn't so much want an occupation as an instant social scene and the bigger the names, the better. Was she contemplating keeping the business going in order to meet those supposed big names?

'I haven't studied the names, Mrs Mundell, I'm sorry. Being from Newcastle they wouldn't mean much to me probably,' Rosalie said hoping the temporising ploy would do.

'Eh, Lass, you could just bring the diary through and me and the wife could soon tell you who's who.' Will Mundell was very pleased with this thought and sent his wife a broad smile.

Rosalie spluttered and was grateful for the intervention of Lauren. 'She can't do that, Dad,' the girl said, 'Client confidentiality. We know about that, don't we, Ted?'

'Course, we do. Listen, Dad, Lauren thinks we should be looking at a villa on the Algarve.'

'Does she now? And whose money is she spending on that? We haven't seen the best of this place yet, have we? And what about the gardens? I hear there're some prize-winning rhododendrons in that there gorge.' He gestured towards the river which could be picked out by the line of trees growing along its banks.

Rosalie did look at Agnes then and saw the shock on the older woman's face. David had promised the gorge wasn't included in the sale. She turned to David and he shook his head imperceptibly. So, he was now playing along. These lottery winners weren't in with any chance of buying Maldington House.

'I was out in the garden this morning, Mr Mundell. Bob, our gardener is very knowledgeable and supplies the house with most of the produce we need from the walled garden.' Rosalie sent Betty a warm smile.

'That right!' Mrs Mundell said. 'I hope he don't keep no hens?'

'No, there's a local supply of eggs and several farms send in fresh poultry and other meat and game,' Rosalie said.

'And are you into re-cycling?' Mrs Mundell crossed her arms over her ample chest and Rosalie decided she'd rather work in a burger bar than stay on here if there was even the remotest prospect of this woman being in charge.

'The kitchen has a slops pail,' David intervened. 'We have the pigsty in the grounds, of course, up beside gardener's cottage.' He ignored Mrs Mundell's horrified gasp and signalled to the leader of the minders that they should be moving on.

With seamless coordination, the party was moved out of the Peacock Room and along the corridor to the drawing room. Rosalie sank onto a chair and saw Betty do the same.

'I think Bob and me had better put our names on the council waiting list,' Betty said quietly, 'For a house. I expect you'll be going back to Newcastle, Rosalie?'

'I can't see David selling his house to this group,' Rosalie replied. 'I think they'd lost the purchase by the time he mentioned the pigsty.'

Betty grinned. 'Of course. We haven't had a pig in it in my time. I'm not sure even Bob's dad had them. Mrs Mundell looked scunnered at the prospect.'

Rosalie grinned back. 'I'll help you clear up.'

★ ★ ★

Rosalie marvelled at the impassive faces both David and Agnes maintained as they came into the kitchen nearly an hour later. However, as soon as the people carriers were powering down the front drive, spraying gravel into the lawns, the façade crumbled and she could see peace was endangered.

'Excuse me a moment, will you?' David asked, and the formality of his tone told Rosalie all she needed to know.

She didn't get any chance to ask Agnes how the rest of the visit had gone before he reappeared with the saggy carrier bag of sawdust. He dropped it onto the kitchen table.

'Anybody got any ideas?' David's heightened colour and the furious energy he was keeping contained in his long-muscled frame was daunting, if not scary. Rosalie said nothing but Agnes was made of less feeble fibre.

'Oh, thank you, I couldn't remember where I'd left that. Where did you find it?' Agnes asked with complete disregard for the truth or anything approaching the truth. Rosalie cringed as David's steely gaze flashed between her and his mother. She kept silent.

'Really, Mother? I'm supposed to believe you were up in the attics poking around under the eaves when I cannot remember you ever having gone there?' He shifted his weight from one foot to the other. Rosalie heard Betty pause in her loading of the dishwasher. 'I cannot recall any time you've gone up there to store something or take something out of storage. It's always been Dad or me.'

'So, are you saying you found it in the attics, dear?' Agnes persisted.

'No, I am not saying that.'

'Then why are we discussing the attics?' Agnes sat down and gazed up at her son whose face was now suffused in red. The tie he'd worn for the formal visitation seemed to be in danger of choking him.

David turned his attention to Betty and Rosalie. He glanced from one to the other but focussed his attention on Rosalie.

'Mea Culpa,' Rosalie said, and Agnes sighed. Betty shut the dishwasher with a clatter of crockery and sped out into the courtyard. Within seconds the tang of cigarette smoke hung in the air.

'Childish after all,' David swept up his folder of papers, 'And ultimately ineffectual. They're going to instruct a survey.' The ladies heard him address a remark to Betty as he passed her in the yard. The housekeeper came back in and Rosalie thought she looked uneasy.

'I'm really sorry, Mrs Logie. I spotted a trickle of sawdust in the mezzanine cloaks and when I saw it led to the Hope Chest, I opened it and took the bag out.' Betty said. 'I really meant to go back for it, but Wyn called down to me just at the wrong moment. She needed a hand straightening the quilt on the Super-King.'

'Don't worry, Betty. He didn't allow the visitors much chance to inspect the stuff Rosalie had carefully planted in the attics. I wasn't there, of course. As he said, I don't go up that rickety closed stair, but I could hear most of what was said through the open door.'

'How did David explain it?' Rosalie asked.

'Quite clever actually,' Agnes conceded with a grin that might have been pride in her son's quick thinking. 'He said we'd had some of the local school children up there doing a bit of carpentry in situ.'

'Clever indeed,' Rosalie agreed. 'Sorry, it was a silly idea in the first place.' She was consumed by embarrassment and knew she'd have to go to Carriage House as soon as possible and apologise to David.

'Nonsense, my dear. It lets David know there's real opposition to his plan and we won't be steam-rollered.' She glanced at the kitchen clock. 'Betty, it's time you headed off. This is Tuesday, drama tonight.'

'Thank you, Mrs Logie. Will I see you this evening, Rosalie? Bob doesn't fancy the play, but I've got a ticket.'

'Yes, I'm being treated by Tam and Sadie so I can meet some of the neighbours.' Rosalie had thought she might give it a miss, but it would be good to go along and support Betty. 'I'll drive the house car down to the village, so I'll pick you up outside your cottage.'

'I'll be there, too. That's what I was going to tell you earlier, Rosalie. Your young man is coming along, although he'll be travelling with Rick and Hazel.' Agnes smiled as if she'd delivered news Rosalie was waiting for.

'I . . . '

'Yes, I know, he isn't your young man. Anyway, he's charmingly attentive to older ladies like me,' Agnes said with a twinkle in her eye. Rosalie bit her tongue. She'd just offered to drive them all down to the village. It wasn't possible to withdraw.

11

David pulled the motor over in a side street and killed the engine. The community theatre venue in Wolcester was in the centre of the town, but he'd walk forward the few hundred yards to the square. He knew there'd be little hope of parking on the square as he'd cut his arrival time quite close to curtain up and all the available spaces would be gone.

He became aware of a pain in his hands and when he looked down, realised he was gripping the steering wheel as if it would be wrenched from him at any moment. He sighed.

'This is all to do with you, Rosalie Garden. You and your petty games with bags of sawdust,' he said aloud to the empty vehicle. People hurrying past on the pavement didn't stop to look at the madman talking to himself and he was fleetingly grateful for that. Reports taken back to his mother or his sister-in-law,

Chris, might be difficult to refute.

He'd puzzled over the afternoon's events until his mind was in turmoil. Of course he'd known Agnes was opposed to selling up, but he couldn't think why Rosalie had jumped on the platform. Her contract, which he'd had the business lawyer check over, was for seven months. She would hardly be affected in any way by a sale. She was nobody's fool and he knew she'd realised as soon as he mentioned the pigsty that he wouldn't be selling Maldington to the Mundells. 'Even if theirs is the only offer,' he said. It was pleasing that no one argued.

David got out of the car and locked it. Just as he arrived in the square, he heard a familiar voice and a reply in a Newcastle accent.

'Steve, will you be okay for ten minutes if I go and have a word with my Aunty Bea?' Hazel Easton asked and Steve Baxter replied.

'Go ahead, lovey. I've met some of the folks from Maldington now and I see they're getting out of a minibus across there.'

David followed the line of Steve's out-stretched arm to where his mother, Betty and Rosalie were grouping themselves as they came out of the bus. He caught his breath at the picture Rosalie presented. Even just a week of regular hours, good sleep and a proper diet was beginning to make a difference. Her skin glowed with health and her hair, piled up in an untidy bun, was a lustrous mass.

David watched Steve study the group getting down from the minibus. He saw how the other man's eyes narrowed as he watched Rosalie who was easily the most striking looking woman among the others. For the most part the company were grey-haired and anorak clad. Rosalie looked good in a knee-length ruby coloured overshirt and black leggings. In another life, David would have found a chance to let this woman know how striking she was. In another life, he would have resented the proprietorial gaze Steve Baxter fixed on his mother's chef. In another life? Who was he trying to kid? He really was very uncomfortable around Baxter's open and intense interest. There was something not quite right, he felt, and wondered whether Baxter's interest was hostile.

'Where did that come from?' he asked himself.

★ ★ ★

Rosalie's heart flipped a little as she saw Steve come strolling towards the group. Although she'd known to expect him, it was still a shock after eleven months of never seeing him, to keep bumping into him like this. She cast an instinctive glance towards Agnes and Betty.

'Good evening, Ladies,' Steve said as he approached, and Rosalie wondered at the clothes he was wearing. Before he lost his job and her business crashed, he would not have considered wearing a hoodie and jeans. Perhaps his case worker had found things for him.

Her mother had acted as a go-between with Steve's mother at the time they were ejected from the flat and business premises. She knew from snatches of conversation her mother had had with Mrs Baxter, that everything he owned had gone to their creditors, or simply gone. Who knew what happened to things in the darkest days of an addiction?

'Steve,' Agnes said, 'How nice of you to come along. I hope you won't be disappointed because I know you city types like a more sophisticated drama than the one our local rep will be offering.'

'Don't know about that,' Steve said, and Rosalie's insides clenched as he simpered. When did a grown man simper? Only when he was after something, she thought.

'Don't listen to Mrs Logie,' Betty said, 'She's the one who likes to go into the city, to the Sage or the Theatre Royal. The rest of us love these Agatha Christie adaptations.'

Rosalie watched as Steve turned his head towards the housekeeper and smiled. 'Do you manage to work out 'who dunnit', then?'

'Goodness, no,' Betty said, 'And I'm sure if they did the same book every time, I still wouldn't remember.'

Rosalie was aware that Agnes was scanning the crowd and remembered the older woman had said she wanted to make contact with some folk in the interval. Agnes gave a tiny squeak and, with fleeting apologies to the rest of them, headed towards some well-dressed business types who were congregating in the entrance. Rosalie was sure that Mr Waugh's partner was among them.

'Friends?' Steve asked, but neither Rosalie nor Betty replied directly. There might not be any feudal overtones in their employment relations these days, but there was still a reticence to discuss each others' business.

'Oh, Mrs Logie knows everyone,' Betty said cheerfully. 'Could you excuse me, too? I see Hazel and her Aunty Bea. Aunty Bea needs a bit of help with that huge garden around her cottage and Bob has said he'll do some tidying up for her.

I said to Bob I'd fix a date.'

'Country life seems to be a whirlwind of activity,' Steve said to Rosalie once they were alone. She was conscious of his stare. It was intent, lingering on her face as if he was starved of her company. How dare he come here and threaten her new life? How dare he make her feel it would be a good idea to run away, back to her parents and work in a school canteen somewhere?

She didn't reply and when Steve stretched out a hand to catch her arm, she stepped away from him.

'Don't try the Lady Muck attitude with me, Rosalie. I've nothing else to lose since you let the business go under,' he hissed at her. Low enough to prevent anyone else making sense of it, but loud enough for her to hear.

'Really, Steve?' Rosalie said, goaded into a response. 'I let the business go under? Haven't the counsellors and mentors made you face up to reality yet?'

'The reality is that I gave you a family heirloom on the basis we would be together, and it would pass down through the generations as it has done already . . . '

'What?' Rosalie asked scornfully. 'Are you on about that ring again? Is that why you're here, deceiving that nice cousin of yours and his wife?'

'That ring is worth many thousands of pounds and I want it back. I have two nieces, you know.' Rosalie wondered if there was a touch of madness in Steve's tone. His gaze never left her face and she knew he was past reasoning with.

'Good evening,' David Logie said, nodding to them both. Rosalie hadn't thought she'd be glad to see the man quite so soon, but circumstances meant she was.

'David,' she said. 'Agnes didn't say you'd be here tonight.' She saw the flash of intent in David's eyes, but it was gone in an instant.

'She didn't know. I didn't myself, but Libby's nephews are involved in this play and their mum had got me an opening night ticket. Where is Mum?' Before

Rosalie could reply, Steve answered.

'She saw some pals, David, and headed off into the foyer with them. Look, perhaps you two wouldn't mind, but I need to catch Hazel and Rick. They have my ticket.' He gave them a wave and sprinted across the square to catch up with the group as they disappeared into the theatre.

'Do you miss him?' David asked and Rosalie turned a startled look in his direction. What on earth had given him that idea?

'Miss him?' she parroted. 'Oh yes, and it's been one of the few positives of this last year, knowing that Steve would still be missing when I woke up in the morning.'

'I beg your pardon,' David said with what sounded like injured dignity, 'I thought from your stricken expression you wanted him to stay with you.'

Ah, Rosalie thought. I probably did look stricken, but it's because of the damage the man can do, not because I miss him.

'Sorry. No.' She shuffled from one foot to the other. If she was going to apologise for her part in the sawdust spreading, this might be the only chance she'd get. 'I should also say sorry for the ridiculous plot with the sawdust.'

'Should you?' David's expression was unreadable. Rosalie could see a couple in their thirties approaching them along the pavement.

'Yes. It was childish and it was never going to put off any serious surveyor.' There, she'd said it. The couple were on top of them now.

'David,' the man said and threw an arm around his shoulders.

'Matt, hi. Chris,' David said and turned to catch the woman in a bear hug. 'This is Rosalie Garden who has joined mum's business as the resident chef.'

Rosalie shook hands with them and was about to go off to hunt for Sadie and Tam when they heard the warning bell ringing out from the foyer.

'Last as usual,' Chris said and led them forward into the theatre. 'You won't have

154

been before, Rosalie. It's unreserved seating and tonight they're performing in the round. Maybe David said — both our sons are in this production.'

They settled into a row. Rosalie waved to her hosts who weren't too far away, and the theatre lights went black. Sitting so close to David, she was aware of his even breathing and after a moment or two, of his distinctive smell. It was a mix of a strong herb-based soap and dog. It occurred to her that she'd been conscious of it for a couple of days now. It was stronger than the lingering aroma of fresh coffee he carried everywhere, too.

She smiled in the darkness. Her muscles relaxed and within a quarter of an hour she was wrapped up in the mystery unfolding on stage.

* * *

Rosalie blinked as the interval lights came on. Chris and Matt made their apologies, but they had backstage passes and were desperate to congratulate their sons. They smiled encouragingly at David as they disappeared towards the backstage area.

Rosalie could see David wanted to know exactly what it was Agnes was up to, but as she had disappeared in the crowd, he had little hope of finding her in the short break. They sat still. Sadie and Tam waved as they, too, headed backstage.

'We don't really appear to be in with the in-crowd,' David said, and Rosalie glanced at him. She thought he looked strained.

'No, we don't. Do either of the boys remind you of Libby?'

'Not really. They take after Matt's side of their family. Libby was fair-haired with freckles. Matt is dark as you can see, and he goes quite brown whenever the sun comes out.' David spoke slowly as if he was thinking about it for the first time. 'But, you know, they do sometimes have an aspect of her. A look or a gesture reminds me.'

'Do you find that hard?'

'A bit, but not a lot and I don't avoid them, if that's where this is heading.'

'No, no, sorry. I didn't mean to probe . . . '

'Of course you didn't. It's me who should be apologising. I'm still wound up about that tour this morning,' David said and grimaced. 'Are all the prospective buyers going to be so eccentric? I just couldn't see those people handling Bob and Betty, or even Wyn and Keith, at all well.'

'No.' Rosalie wondered whether this was the moment to mention Bob's confidence about Betty's education. She decided that sooner was probably better. 'Bob told me Betty doesn't read very well. I can see how that would make it hard for her to get another suitable job around the area.'

'Ah, did he?'

'I've been thinking about it. I'll try to watch how Betty picks information up and do the same, but I could also do something with colours, maybe. Like different coloured lids on storage boxes.'

'I suppose I did think new owners would keep the staff, but who knows. It's kind of you to think of helping Betty. There is a one-to-one adult tutor in Wolcester and Bob has been trying to get Betty to sign up with her for ages.' David moved restlessly in his seat. 'Betty doesn't see the need, but it would help her enormously.'

★ ★ ★

Later Rosalie drove Betty home from the village and turned the car towards the back of the big house. A figure crossed the lower drive and within seconds the estate dogs raced after it. Rosalie took a steadying breath. She realised she'd thought it might be Steve and without anyone else around was a little nervous.

David was waiting outside the kitchen door when she drove into the yard and killed the headlights. The dogs lay about or moved slowly around the narrow borders testing all the smells they could pick up there and bringing the security lighting on. She breathed in the night smells humans could register and watched a couple of bats sweeping the sky above them. This was all becoming familiar and Rosalie knew it was going to be very difficult leaving it whether that was at the end of her contract or earlier if David found a buyer who wanted early entry.

In the glare of the security lights, she could see he looked uptight and irritated. She unlocked the house.

'Where is my mother?' he asked as they went into the kitchen. He strode over to the coffee machine and set it in motion, taking out mugs and milk as he waited for an answer. Rosalie didn't miss the tense set of his shoulders even through the light tweed jacket he was wearing.

'She was invited to have a little supper with some of the people she met up with and Mr Craig is going to drive her back,' Rosalie said.

'Alastair Craig? Huh. I might have known.' David went out into the yard and Rosalie heard him securing the dogs in some kennels there. He came back in, bringing cold air and even more frustration, if that was

159

possible. Pausing inside the back door, he heeled off his wellies.

'Who is Alastair Craig?' she asked. 'Would you like some chocolate cake?'

'Yes please,' David said, 'I know which question is more important.' He shrugged off his jacket and hung it over a chair back. 'Let's take this through to the snug before I answer your other one.'

The snug was a small sitting-room off the front vestibule. It was kept locked while there were paying guests in the house, but Rosalie had been in it once or twice. Agnes enjoyed having her morning coffee there.

'Alastair Craig is a business friend of Reuben Waugh's. He would like to buy into the house and help Mum run it as she does, but he'd also like to install other up-to-date features. Maybe a spa facility,' David said once they were settled in the snug. Rosalie had kicked off her shoes and settled into a squashy settee with her legs curled under her bottom and her coffee mug on the side-table.

'A spa facility?' she said, testing the

theory as she spoke the words. 'Would you think about a swimming pool?'

'It isn't going to happen, Rosalie. Personally, I think Alastair's interest is in my mother, and not in becoming a hotelier.' David stretched his legs and hooked a stool dragging it across the floor so he could put his feet up. He took a long drink from his coffee mug and closed his eyes.

'Ah,' Rosalie said. 'I see.' She sipped her own coffee which was still hot even with the milk she'd added. How David managed to swallow quite so much in one go was beyond her understanding.

'Do you?' David's eyes snapped open and he fixed her with an intent gaze that made her wonder if she should apologise for something.

'Well, the Doig twins were teasing her last week about how glamorous she looked the night the Waughs invited her to eat with them. Marcus implied . . . '

'She ought to fire those two,' David interrupted with a growl. 'Marcus is too outspoken for anybody's good.'

'Really? They're very good at the job and Agnes did say how much she appreciated their company after . . . ' Rosalie tailed off. How could she have landed herself in this?

'After Libby died,' David finished for her. 'Yes, they saved our sanity then, it's true.' He finished his coffee and peered into the mug. Rosalie wondered if he was checking for any he might have missed. 'You don't have to tiptoe around it, Rosalie. Time passes and of course, it was always in our future. There was never any hope of a cure that would arrive in time for Libby.'

'You mean it didn't come as a surprise?' she asked.

'Exactly. Whereas perhaps you were surprised to discover Steve had a problem with alcohol? He must have been hiding it to start with?' David asked with a quiet sincerity. People often took it for granted that a drink problem was always obvious, so Rosalie was grateful for his insight.

'Hiding in plain sight, I suppose, but

yes, he did.' She set her unfinished coffee down and slid her feet onto the floor. 'Unexplained cash crises, duvet days and the odd morning when his car wasn't where it should be.'

'Most young people would be able to say the same,' David said.

'Most young people start becoming older people once the idea of being a student, but with a salary, fades into the reality of being an adult. Steve never really got into that groove.' She moved over to the window and peered out through the fronds of ivy into a dark country night.

'No? What about his flat? Didn't he have a mortgage?'

'We decided it would make sense to live above the business kitchens, or at least above the offices. We had work done and created a lovely flat,' she sighed. The memory of those heady days of creating things still haunted her dreams and sometimes her waking hours, too.

They'd hammered out a plan with an architect and a builder and Steve had a client who specialised in bathroom fittings. Curiously, the flat didn't have a real kitchen as they'd decided to eat the trial meals Rosalie was creating for the business. There was a kitchenette with a sink, a microwave and a kettle.

They'd decided, she gave a tiny bitter laugh. Steve had told her.

'God, woman, don't think I want to wait all night for you to perfect something when there's plenty of leftovers filling the fridges downstairs. No kitchen. Let's remove your temptation to keep cooking.'

It wasn't the first of his pronouncements, but on reflection, it was the boldest. He was testing her, wasn't he? How far could he push her away from what she loved and still have her in his hold?

The shivering began then as it often did. The memory of how Steve had put everything that might be lost as collateral into her name, caused an icy shiver to surround her heart and squeeze the muscle so she trembled. And it had been used as collateral, but by him forging her signature over and over, so she lost it all.

'Rosalie,' David's voice held an urgency that made her turn to face him. She gave a shaky little laugh. 'Rosalie, you're trembling.' He crossed the room and slid an arm around her.

'Sorry, I'm sorry.' She tried to pull out of his hold, but somehow the will wasn't in her effort and he was lifting her off her feet to set her back down in the settee. He dropped beside her and took her into his arms.

'Why would you be sorry?'

'Because I was a fool and there's no reason why you or anyone should have to clear it all up,' she said through tears. David's hand struggled into the pocket of his chinos and he hauled out a hanky. She accepted it and mopped up the mess.

'Who did come to your rescue?'

'My dad. I owe my dad a lot of money. That's why I need to keep my job. His loan to me has left him and mum in straitened circumstances.'

'Ah,' David said. 'Hence the shenanigans with the sawdust.' He sighed, and Rosalie sniffed. She blew her nose.

'Look, I am sorry. Just, please, do not expect me to welcome Steve Baxter or celebrate his supposed recovery.' She tried to stand up, but her overshirt was caught beneath David's thigh and she couldn't pull it clear. He rolled to the right onto his other thigh, but that only made her sink further into the squashy cushions Agnes favoured throughout the house.

'Rosalie,' David murmured as he turned back towards her and brought his head down. His lips closed over hers in a kiss of exquisite tenderness that soon burned into a fire of longing and hunger. A few startled seconds were all it took to make her realise she wanted this, too, and return his kiss with heated fervour.

12

Rosalie turned over in her bed. Wakened by something, she lay for a moment or two listening. Voices floated up the internal staircase from the kitchen below: local voices speaking at a normal level. Agnes, perhaps, and a male voice, she thought at last. There was a deep and rich male voice answering her employer.

It was dark in the room and there was little noise from the grounds. Night animals and hunting birds raised a screech from time to time, but even that was minimal. She turned again and gnawed the back of her hand as she used to do when she was a little girl and the world seemed an unfriendly place for some reason. Across the room the power light on the television developed a red halo. She closed her eyes and slept.

When Rosalie woke again, natural light flooded her room. She lay on her back and stretched. Had she dreamed that Agnes came into the room last night with a strange man? It took a moment or two for the sleepy mists to break up and she remembered clearly how she'd been wakened by voices; but from the kitchen. Not her room.

David had not come into her room either.

She had asked him to, but he'd shaken his head and left, stumbling as he tried to pull on his wellies while moving and calm the dogs which reacted to the noise he was making with frenzied barking.

He left her after the most exciting kiss she'd shared with anyone, ever. He didn't want to take it any further, she thought with a touch of bitterness. She trembled. The intensity of feeling she'd experienced shook her, even now in the clear light of a summer morning. Goosebumps lifted across her skin. Hadn't it been the same for him, she wondered sadly. Why did she choose the wrong men? Even when they were so obviously the right ones?

She threw back the duvet.

Needles of bitter cold pinged off her skin as she stood under the shower. She watched her arms turning bright pink in the shocking temperature and shivered as the muscles of her legs contracted in reaction. The soap didn't foam under the cold onslaught and, eventually, she turned the temperature control to a more normal level.

Downstairs, Rosalie was breakfasted and wondering what to do next when Agnes appeared in the kitchen doorway. She saw the older woman's slightly embarrassed smile and raised a sympathetic eyebrow.

'Morning, Agnes. I see your lift brought you home safely,' Rosalie said and mentally berated herself. Could she possibly sound more coy? More like her mother?

'He did, but he was only here briefly. I do hope we didn't waken you, my dear, Alastair has a rather loud voice. He was a football referee in another life.'

'Goodness, no,' Rosalie lied. Well, she'd only been awake for three or four minutes at the most. It didn't count. 'What time did you come in?'

'I'm not sure I want to answer that,' Agnes said with a smile in her voice that cheered Rosalie up. 'Oh look, here's David.'

Rosalie felt the blood drain from her face and wished she'd paid more attention to the tell-tale footsteps coming across the yard. They must have alerted Agnes. She didn't feel at all equal to a confrontation with David.

On the other hand, she'd done nothing wrong. It was David who'd kissed her and then bottled out of the challenge when she responded to him.

'Morning, Mum, Rosalie,' David said as he put his document wallet on the table without making eye contact with either lady. Rosalie watched him take yesterday's note out from under the dolphin fridge magnet and slide a fresh one in. Her gaze lingered a little on the length of his artist's fingers with a new knowledge of their seductive strength. They'd held her head in a secure clasp while he kissed her ruthlessly.

'Are you staying with Bernie and Hamish tonight?' Agnes asked.

'Yes, Bernie is always very keen to feed me, and as Hamish has a bottle open before I know it, it's safer to stay over. Besides, I've got several of the contractors who are lined up to work on their steading conversion booked in for site visits. I don't know if they can all make it today.' He did look round at her then, but Rosalie pretended to be absorbed with a crate of potatoes Bob had left for inspection. 'One or two might have to come tomorrow morning.'

'You'll be on your own then, Rosalie, because I've accepted an invitation to play bridge with Alastair and a couple of his neighbours.' Agnes sounded concerned.

'That's fine, Agnes. Bob and Betty are no distance away and I'll lock the door, too, if you remember to take a key,' Rosalie said. She wasn't worried about being on her own despite the size of the house. It was a warm and lived in home. However, she very much did not want Steve to walk in again as he'd done over the weekend. That was one surprise she'd prefer to do without. David hesitated as he lifted his documents. 'I'm really sorry I can't guarantee being back, Rosalie. This commission is so close to the start of the work that I need to make sure all the contractors are clued up and geared up.'

'You don't live in the house,' Rosalie said with such a sharp edge Agnes glanced from one to the other. Rosalie could have kicked herself. How stupid was she being sending that kind of message for Agnes to pick up on?

'No, I don't, but the carriage house is a mite nearer to hand than Bob's cottage.' He straightened and Rosalie had to meet a challenging glare. How dare he, she thought, after he kissed me so seductively but abandoned me. 'I have arranged for the second lot of prospective buyers to tour the house tomorrow — in the afternoon.' He turned away from her then to speak directly to Agnes, 'I hope you can be here, Mum.'

'Yes, of course,' Agnes replied, and Rosalie's heart was torn by the defeat in her voice. 'Perhaps Rosalie will make some more of her scones. They went down well with the lottery winners.'

'I'm not confident we'll be hearing from them,' David said as he shucked back his sleeve to glance at the time on his watch. 'The young woman was fairly over-awed by the scale of everything. I heard her whispering to her husband about how you needed to be born into this kind of property to do it justice.'

Rosalie was a little taken aback by this observation. She'd thought the young woman was simply nervous, but that remark made her sound more sensible and sensitive than her in-laws.

'Really?' Agnes replied. 'Perceptive of her. Who are tomorrow's lot?'

'They're representing some investment capitalists. Looking to get into the leisure market, I believe,' David said. 'Seems as if Alastair Craig isn't the only person who thinks the guest house needs to be a spa.'

He crossed the room and drew his mother into a hug. 'Please, Mum, don't fret. You will have your rhoddies and nothing will happen during this season of bookings, I promise.'

'You'd better get going,' Agnes said and gave him a gentle push.

* * *

'Do I detect a little edge between you two this morning?' Agnes asked Rosalie as they heard David's big car leaving the yard.

Rosalie hesitated a fraction too long and could see her eventual response raised more questions in Agnes's mind than it answered. She was going to have to get a grip on this. Everybody knew sleeping with your employer, or her son, was a bad, bad idea. Doesn't stop one wanting, though, was the unbidden reply that snapped into Rosalie's mind. She rubbed the earth off a potato with her thumb.

'Nothing to worry about, Agnes,' she said, 'A tiny misunderstanding.'

'I hope he isn't persecuting you over that benighted sawdust?'

'No, not at all,' Rosalie said. 'Look at these wonderful potatoes Bob has dug. Pity we don't have any guests this week.'

She watched the speculative gaze Agnes cast over the crate of potatoes and knew the older lady would be coming back to the issue, if not now, then certainly later.

'I'm going down to see Tam Anscomb again this morning. If you put most of the potatoes into the back of the car, I'll get him to sell them on for Bob.'

Rosalie was sitting at the kitchen table with a mug of coffee and Dougie's log-book of menus. She'd seen from the diary that they would be hosting a very large wedding reception in three weeks' time and was interested to know how Dougie had approached that kind of event.

There were seven similar occasions documented and the first things she noticed were the buying in of some of the catering and the employment of extra staff. She flicked through the staff diary and saw that the Doig twins and Keith Brodie were already signed up together with Betty, Wyn and Bob for their forthcoming one and Rosalie said, 'Thank the Lord.'

'Well. I don't know about that, Rosalie, but I'm here anyway,' Betty said as she came through from the house. 'Wyn's gone out from the basement to bring the laundry in.' The housekeeper went over to switch on the kettle, shaking the biscuit tin as she passed it.

'I'm starting to plan for the big wedding we have in three weeks' time. I was glad to see Keith will be helping in the kitchen,' Rosalie said over her shoulder. 'I must be getting old, but I do miss having a kitchen porter when it's one of his off days.' Wyn came down the steps into the kitchen at that moment.

'Morning, Rosalie. David's jacket was hanging on the back of the chair you're sitting on when I came in earlier. I took it across and hung it on the outside handle of his front door.' Wyn slipped across to the biscuit tin and sent Betty a conspiratorial smile. 'Not like him. He usually covers his tracks better than that.'

Rosalie felt her face fire with embarrassment, but the others were deep in a discussion about the flavoured shortbreads she'd added to the biscuit tin and perhaps didn't notice. She waited until they joined her at the table with their coffees before asking what Wyn meant.

'He pops over from time to time through the night if he thinks Mrs L might be upset about anything,' Wyn said.

'Yes, she can be a bit highly strung,' Betty added, 'And David doesn't think Mr Craig should keep on at her about turning the business into a spa.'

'Oh, I see,' Rosalie said, and she did. The ladies thought Agnes might have had a difficult evening with Alastair Craig. She kept to herself the fact he'd been here through the night, too. She didn't see any point in creating speculation.

'I enjoyed chatting to your Steve,' Betty

said, and it caught Rosalie off-guard. She'd been so immersed in whether Agnes had a relationship with Alastair Craig, she'd allowed the continuing threat of Steve's presence in the area to slip past.

'He's not my Steve,' she said firmly.

'Oh, I don't know about that, Rosalie, give the bloke a chance. He's followed you all the way out here when he could be applying for accountancy jobs in Newcastle,' Betty said, and Rosalie saw Wyn's eyebrows lift in surprise.

'Accountancy, eh?' Wyn said, 'And he's here driving the eggs around? Sounds like something to me.'

Rosalie was at a loss to know what to say. On the one hand, it didn't matter what anyone thought about her relationship with Steve, except for David of course, but on the other; she did want to prevent Betty and Wyn succumbing to his charm. If he fell off the wagon while he was still here, they might be tempted into lending him cash. Loans they'd never see repaid.

'You have to understand that Steve

has a bit of a problem with his drink,' she said slowly. 'It led to things between us getting difficult and then fracturing.'

'Some people try really hard to get back on track.'

'I know they do Betty, but I'm afraid I don't think Steve is in that category. I think he's come here to cause mischief.' In fact, she knew he had because he'd said as much in that phone call: when people know what a thief they have in their nest, he'd said.

13

David eased the car through the gates into the yard. He glanced up at Rosalie's window and saw there was a light on. Was she still awake or had she gone to sleep with it on? He'd noticed once or twice how late she sometimes seemed to be up and how early she rose.

The dogs were secured in the kennels and there was a lot of whimpering and movement from inside, but he didn't go over to them. They knew his smell and didn't bark. In fact they didn't normally react to his arrival at all, when they'd been walked and fed by Bob. David looked around to see if there was a deer or a fox slinking around. He saw the gate into the kitchen garden was standing open. He lifted the heavy flashlight from the passenger footwell and got out of the car as quietly as he could.

Just as he was wondering how hard you had to hit someone with a flashlight to knock them out, but not kill them, Rosalie came into the yard from the garden.

'It's you,' he said, 'So I don't need to put myself in danger of a manslaughter charge.' He waved the flashlight. 'I noticed the dogs were a bit restless.' He felt his heart constrict as he studied the drawn lines around her eyes and the downward tilt of her mouth. He was trying to think the best of Steve Baxter, but at moments like this when he saw how vulnerable Rosalie could look, it was impossible. What right had the man to turn up in her new existence and try to inveigle himself into everybody's good graces? Why was he here?

'I wasn't sleeping and when your mother came in, I gave up trying. She said this morning that Alastair Craig had been a football referee. He was in full flow tonight about what cards they should have played in some rubber or other.' Rosalie glanced back into the garden and David was captivated by the way her beautiful hair swung, thick and heavy across her shoulders. 'I love the smells of the night garden and its slight feeling of otherworldliness.'

'Yes, it's only a month until Midsummer. There are a lot of flowers in bloom.' He shifted the flashlight from his right hand to his left and clicked it on. 'Have you walked into the little wood in the dark? There's a small summer-house and a pond.' He turned away from her and sent the beam from his torch over towards a path that snaked out of the yard and under the mature trees beyond the old carriage house and stable buildings. 'Want to take a look?'

He saw the way she hesitated, and guilt thumped him in the gut. How could he have left her last night when it was he who'd kissed her? Yet again, he reminded himself of the teenager he'd been — arrogant and scared witless at the same time.

'I promise I won't . . . '

'I know, David. Business and pleasure, eh?' She pulled the zip on her tracksuit jacket up unintentionally drawing his attention to the pyjama top underneath, and set off onto the path. David watched the rigid set of her shoulder muscles and sighed. Who was he kidding? Rosalie Garden was well and truly under his skin.

'All quiet here, this evening, apart from the retired football referee?' he asked after he caught up with her. They were skirting the edge of a small conifer plantation and the pond he'd mentioned was in view.

'Yes, it was actually. Bob came by about ten and saw to the dogs.' David watched as Rosalie lifted a small stone or two and sent them into the pond with tiny plops that sounded loud in the night-time. He could just make out the ripples in the light from his torch, but they weren't distinct.

An owl flew low over the cleared ground around the water and a piercing shriek filled the air as it sank its claws into something small and squirming.

'Oh dear,' Rosalie said, 'I might not be cut out for country living after all.'

David felt a tiny bubble of excitement well in his gut. Did her remark mean she'd been considering a more permanent move from the city, he wondered.

'If Steve weren't in the picture, do you think you might find country living attractive?' David asked. 'If I ever succeed in getting a client past Mum's shenanigans, you'd want another position of course, but there are good quality jobs around.'

'I don't know yet,' Rosalie answered. 'I am enjoying having a kitchen again, that's certainly true.'

'And I think the kitchen is enjoying having you.'

'What do you mean? Dougie was a great chef by all accounts and I'm finding his record-keeping very helpful as I try to plan the bigger events coming up,' Rosalie said generously.

'He didn't look anything like as fetching in his pyjamas,' David said.

'David Logie! I have got a tracksuit on on top.' He watched a war of emotions crease her face and it turned out she was trying to stop herself asking him why he was selling up his inheritance. It came out so abruptly, David was taken by surprise.

'Why do you want to give all this up?' she asked.

He knew the arguments he'd rehearsed over and over among the family. His cousins and his aunts had cross questioned him relentlessly when he first started asking around, testing the market. The house was too big. His mother wasn't getting any younger. The gardens could be split with an option for the successful buyer to take them on when Agnes decided to hang up her trowel. Watching Rosalie watch him, they didn't seem so clear.

'I can't face the idea of living in the house without Libby,' he said baldly, but it didn't deter Rosalie.

'You never did live in the house with her, though.'

David sighed. He never did.

'No, we didn't want to push Mum out before she was ready to move. It's also true that Libby's illness was easier to manage on the ground floor of carriage house. I suppose I thought that I would move into the house with my wife and that children would follow,' he said and was aware that Rosalie still looked sceptical. 'The children might, would probably, have been adopted.'

'I did check out the problems Libby must have faced, and I discovered that fertility could be one of them. I'm so sorry, David,' she said. She still had a handful of little stones and threw them in a bunch into the pool. 'Life is full of disappointments . . .'

'Disillusionment, too,' David answered. He had a momentary vision of the lottery winners as the younger people in their family discovered that having a fortune could bring problems with it. 'I found myself feeling for the younger Mrs Mundell.'

'Yep! She reminded me of Lizzie Bennet in that wonderful scene at Netherfield Park when Mrs Bennet gets worked up and declares they know over twenty families to dine with,' Rosalie agreed and she sent him a smile of such warmth, it made the breath catch in his throat.

'Exactly,' he managed to say.

'What brought you back tonight? You seemed to be sure there would be work carrying over to tomorrow at the building site.'

David hesitated. What had brought him back? He'd eaten supper with his friends but avoided any of the wine Hamish served. Eventually, Bernie had asked him who the lady was, and he'd been covered in confusion. She'd laughed when he replied that he was nervous about allowing his mother the chance to cook up another ploy for his next lot of prospective buyers, maybe seeing the excuse for what it was.

'You,' he said, 'You brought me back.' The flashlight slipped out of his hand into a bush and sent drunken shafts of light around the pool as its weight made the short branches sway. He thought Rosalie's expression wasn't welcoming, but rather a mix of emotions. She was disbelieving but hopeful: reserved but excited. She stood as still as any water nymph encountering a roaming elf and David came to himself.

'I wasn't entirely happy with the idea that Steve might be around while you were alone in the house, although I know I've only come back now.' He tailed off.

'That was a kind thought, but if Steve has been around, I haven't seen him. I am locking the kitchen door outside normal working hours.'

'Good.' He bent down to retrieve his torch and they walked back to the big house.

★ ★ ★

Rosalie thought David would wait while she went in, but he followed her and they both stopped short to see Agnes padding around the kitchen in her dressing-gown.

'Ah, there you are, Rosalie. I saw your lights were on and I wondered if Alastair had disturbed you. It gave me a bit of a jolt to discover you weren't upstairs,'

188

Agnes said.

'Is he still around?' David asked and Rosalie had to stifle a laugh at her employer's outraged expression.

'David, I'm dressed for bed. What did you think?'

'I live in hope that he's going to take you off my hands,' David said and ducked as the tea-towel Agnes was carrying was flicked around his ears.

'Why are you here?' she asked. 'Didn't you say you'd stay over at Highmere?'

'Yes, I did, but I changed my mind. The carpenter did manage to get to the site and Bernie says she can deal with the plasterer in general terms as he's not needed for a few months yet.' Rosalie saw it was a bit of an effort, but David smiled at his mother. 'I really just wanted to be home.'

'You always did as a child. Sleepovers weren't your thing,' Agnes agreed. 'You've brought a smell of damp grass in. Were you up at the pond?'

'Yes, I'd been in the kitchen garden and met David as I came out. We went along the little path.' Rosalie glanced down at her deck shoes and saw she'd picked up a lot of evening dew.

'Alastair headed off after he saw me inside,' Agnes said, and Rosalie kept quiet as she knew Alastair had spent nearly half an hour seeing Agnes safely inside. 'We didn't do very well at the bridge table.'

'Really?' David chipped in, 'Too much gossip, maybe?'

'You know what he's like. He goes on a bit about whatever is consuming him at the minute.'

'Indeed, I do. I expect he was encouraging you about turning the business into a spa again,' David said.

'He was. I can't think it's necessary, though. There are plenty of spa facilities around and we'd just find ourselves competing in a crowded market.' Agnes sighed. 'We do what we offer very well and with our talented new chef,' she smiled at Rosalie, 'I can see us going from strength to strength.' She yawned. 'Bedtime for me.'

'For all of us, I think,' David replied.

'You haven't got any surprises planned for tomorrow's viewers have you?'

Rosalie saw the hasty flush spread up Agnes's neck, but she replied calmly enough.

'I can't think what you mean, my dear. I hope tomorrow's party won't be expecting to have the gorge?'

'Touché, Mum. I haven't included your garden in any particulars. Mundell was pushing his luck.' David retrieved his flashlight from the table where he'd set it down and giving his mum a quick peck on the cheek, he sent Rosalie a salute and left.

Rosalie locked the kitchen door and turned round to find Agnes studying her with an intent gaze. She wondered what was puzzling the older woman.

'Rosalie, Alastair must have woken you. I am sorry. Still, it's lovely to be able to wander around the grounds at night. When David was a wee thing, he didn't sleep at all well. I used to put him into a sling, and we'd take a stroll among the trees.' She sighed. 'Look at the size of him now.'

'Yes,' Rosalie agreed with a laugh, 'It must be strange looking at adult children and thinking things like that.'

'But, you know, if David would only give up this obsession with selling, he'd realise the chance to wander in the night garden with his own children could be a reality,' Agnes said. 'He has at least stopped muttering about 'needing to move on' since you arrived, my dear.'

Rosalie could think of nothing to respond to that and when Agnes turned to the exit said, 'I'll put the lights out.'

She watched Agnes leave the kitchen and heard the door of her private stair close. Quiet descended although not silence. Kitchens always had a fridge or freezer clicking its motor on or off. She switched off the lights and climbed up to bed.

★ ★ ★

When she came down the next morning, Rosalie found David making coffee. He poured some from his first brew for her and set the machine to go again. Agnes came in then and went to the back of the room where Rosalie noticed for the first time that a large red setter was sprawled across the rug in front of the log-burning stove. The dog got up to greet her and Rosalie turned a questioning glance towards David.

'She's called Bracken and she was Libby's special friend,' he said. He took a long drink of coffee and settled a challenging glance on her.

'This is a commercial kitchen, David,' she said.

'We sort of take the view that that bit at the back isn't exactly in the kitchen and allow her to come in here when there aren't any guests in the house.'

Rosalie bit her lip. Hygiene was non-negotiable.

She stirred herself into action and organised the various things she'd learned people ate for breakfast. It gave her something to do while she thought this through. No inspector worthy of the name was going to agree for a nano-second that the back part of the kitchen was anything other than in the kitchen. On the other hand, how often were they going to see an inspector this far out in the wilds? Besides, someone would see them coming through the village and phone ahead. Wouldn't they?

Looking round, she realised how different their breakfasting tastes were. Agnes had some stewed fruit, but no toast. David had a deep bowl of cereal and then helped himself to some left-over cheese sitting in the fridge. She made herself some microwave porridge and tossed seeds and chopped nuts over it.

'Penny for them, Rosalie?' Agnes asked.

'Just musing on how different our breakfasting habits are,' she replied. A wet nose eased up under her elbow and she looked down into a pair of soulful doggy eyes.

'Ah,' David said, 'Bracken likes you.

I was hoping she would. It seems to me she'd be a good companion for you to have around.'

'But the hygiene . . . '

'Sometimes other things are more important than staying in the council's good books,' David said. 'You could always say she's wandered in and you were returning her to the kennels immediately.'

Agnes sent her son a calculating look.

'I have not alerted the council to the presence of a dog in the kitchen, mother,' he said and helped himself to more coffee. 'And I will take her back to the kennels this time.'

14

Checking her own phone for calls from home the previous night had reminded Rosalie that she hadn't heard from either of her parents for three or maybe four days and she took advantage of a quiet half hour to pop up to her room and call them.

The landline rang out, but no one picked up and Rosalie was scrolling through her numbers to find her parents' mobiles when the phone rang.

'Mum,' she said, I was just going to try your mobile.

'That's all right, Dear, it takes me a while to get to the phone and your dad is advised not to do anything in a hurry. I leave it all beside him when I go out, though,' Marie said.

'How are things in Newcastle?' Rosalie asked and was prepared for a long list of snippets about this neighbour and that, but Marie came almost straight to the point. And it wasn't a point Rosalie had been expecting.

'Well, on the hip front, Roger is doing really well. I have to drive the car, but he hasn't murdered me yet. The police would have been in touch, I suppose . . . '

'Mum!' Rosalie laughed, despite her worries. How typical of her mother to go straight to the worst case scenario. 'What other fronts are you reporting on?'

'Oh, my dear, I'm not supposed to tell you. But we've had this enormous bill from the lawyers. Dad thinks he can cover most of it, although not right away,' Marie said and paused.

Rosalie's heart paused, too. The tips of her fingers were so numb that she had to balance her phone on the palm of one hand for a few seconds before she gathered herself and held it back to her ear. She was unsure what to say.

Marie spoke into the silence.

'We thought we'd give up the mobiles meantime as we're mostly in the house and there are one or two subs that could go. Dad won't be able to play any golf this year anyway . . . '

'Mum, I am so sorry. Look I get paid in a week's time and I could send something straight to Smythe and Browne, if that would help.' Rosalie could hear her father stirring in the background and knew her mum had been rumbled. 'I hear Dad. Look, I can send a thousand to the lawyers. I brought some paperwork with me and it'll have their bank details on. It'll be ten days, Mum.'

They talked a little about Roger's health, but Marie was clearly fretting about the trouble she'd got herself into with her husband and Rosalie let her go to try to sort it out. She sat on in her room for a while listening to the birdsong.

Just as she was beginning to understand why David Logie was anxious to sell his house; and just as he was suggesting that she should find other work in the area, this unwelcome sting in the tail of her business failure fell on her. She wondered whether a ton of bricks would have been less damaging.

For now, she had to ensure there was no prospect of Maldington House closing. David might try to reassure her that she would get the length of her contract, but there were so many imponderables. The people coming today had a lot of investment cash behind them. They could easily insist on an early entry. And while Rosalie's skills were transferable, she'd almost certainly have to find living expenses in another job. That would prevent her sending as much cash back to her parents.

Damn Steve Baxter, she thought. Damn him to Hell.

* * *

David arrived in the kitchen around ten to three dressed a little more smartly than usual but looking tired around the eyes. Rosalie felt a twinge of sympathy for him and a tiny twinge of guilt as he'd had a very long day yesterday driving back on her behalf.

'I hope there won't be any sawdust

making people slide around in the attics,' he said, and the tiny twinge of guilt flared into a spasm. Briefly, she wondered whether there was any way she could alert him to the spoof plan to make people think Tam and Sadie were applying for planning permission without landing his mother in deep doo-dah? At the same time, her mother's panicky words on the phone reminded her of the realities of her own situation. She had to keep this work for now.

'You're looking a mite thoughtful,' David said offering her an opening, but somehow the words wouldn't form into any kind of coherent sentence in her brain. 'The sawdust has been swept up, hasn't it?'

'Yes, of course. Betty was up there before you could blink, really,' she said. 'I hope you don't mind, but we agreed she could go into Wolcester this afternoon.'

David raised an eyebrow but didn't say anything making Rosalie a little nervous.

'I saw an advert in the local paper for

a new adult reading group . . .'

'And you persuaded her to go?' David interrupted. He sounded frankly incredulous.

'I did. Why are you so sceptical? Don't you think I have any people skills?'

'What?'

'Sorry, sorry. Steve used to find the worst case outcome for everything I did. I need to remember other people aren't like that,' Rosalie apologised. She felt a tear threaten but took a deep breath and sent David a tentative smile.

'He sounds like a real piece of work. No, my scepticism is down to knowing Betty for most of our lives and having been at school with her — when she got there,' David said. He turned his head towards the back door just as the dogs set up a howl. 'If you've found a way of giving her the confidence to get started, then that's amazing.'

He shifted the document wallet he was carrying from his right hand to his left and gathered Rosalie into a quick hug. She felt a kiss drop onto her hair before he released her.

Outside the dogs' howling reached a crescendo and Rosalie strained to hear if she could distinguish Bracken's call among the others. The setter had gone back to the pack so she wouldn't be in the house while the visitors were being shown around. They heard a couple of vehicles on the gravel of the front path and David moved across the kitchen.

'Where is mother?'

'We're here, David,' she said as she ushered Wyn through the kitchen door. 'The dogs alerted us. Wyn, could you give Rosalie a hand setting up the trolley and serving the afternoon tea?' Agnes picked up the comb she kept beside the handwash sink and drew it through her hair. She took a lipstick from the pocket of her jacket and quickly applied a little before turning back to the others.

* * *

It was getting on towards five o'clock when David, Agnes and the three smart young men from the investment capital-ists arrived in the kitchen. Rosalie was working on some pastry for that night's meal and she didn't hear them come into the room at first. When she turned round she found them standing in a row watching her.

'Rosalie,' David said, 'We enjoyed your scones.'

'Good, I'm glad.' She squinted a little. Afternoon light was flooding the room and showing it to its best advantage. 'Do you have specific questions about the kitchen?' She asked the visitors while rubbing flour off her hands and washing them.

'Not really, chef,' one of them said, 'None of us have worked in catering so we wouldn't know what makes a good kitchen.' He looked round at his col-leagues and they both shook their heads.

'Mind, we know good food when we eat it and the smell wafting into the cor-ridor is pretty spectacular, I think. David says you're quite new in this position,' the youngest one said with a friendly smile.

'Yes. I started here about . . .'

The kitchen door opened and Tam Anscombe walked in interrupting Rosalie's reply. He was wearing a smart blazer with a business shirt underneath and carrying a slender leather briefcase. Rosalie thought how little it took to turn the down-at-heel shopkeeper into an apparently prosperous businessman.

'Beg pardon, folks,' Tam said, blushing slightly. 'I've got a meeting with Mrs Logie about the planning application.'

David sent his mother an enquiring glance which, Rosalie noticed, she affected not to see. Instead she came forward and brought Tam into the company.

'Tam, I had thought the site visit would be completed by now, but the gentlemen were held up by one or two things and so, I'm not quite ready yet. Would you be able to wait for a few minutes?'

'That's not a problem, Mrs Logie. Sadie's well able to manage the shop at this time of day. Did you mention to the gentlemen here about my proposal?'

'Not exactly, no.'

'Right, but it's not confidential and once I lodge the application everyone will know soon enough. It might be politic, though, for the neighbours to hear it from me before that stage. If your firm is looking seriously at buying this house, of course?' he asked the oldest of the three men, probably assuming he was the senior.

'Pete Simmonds,' the young man said and shook hands with Tam. 'What kind of application are you thinking of, Mr . . .'

'Anscombe, but call me Tam. Well, Sadie, that's my wife, and me, we're getting on a bit and running the shop six days a week is hard. Also, we're thinking there'll be a gap in our income if Maldington House is closed for renovations.'

Rosalie risked a quick glance at David and was little surprised to see the puzzlement in his expression.

Pete Simmonds nodded, but kept quiet. 'So, we own the large paddock that runs along your bottom wood, just beyond the tree line,' Tam said and backed up his description by waving an arm in the general direction of where a person might find a wood and a river. 'We thought we might go into re-cycling. Build a plant there. It wouldn't affect the air quality,' he said earnestly.

'But there would be lorry traffic,' Pete Simmonds said thoughtfully, 'Perhaps a lot of it?'

Tam shuffled a bit from foot to foot looking as shifty as any thief caught with the till open. Agnes started to say something, but Tam held a hand up to stop her.

'No, Mrs Logie, this is my responsibility. Yes, there would be lorry traffic. We would start off in a small way and hope to reach maybe two hundred or so lorries a day within three months.' He swung his briefcase up to hold it against his chest. 'The council aren't opposed, but you know what it's like with planning departments. Blow this way one week and that the next.'

'How advanced are these plans, Mr

Anscombe?' one of the other young men asked.

'Well,' Tam said and succeeded in closing down his expression to make it look as if he had all sorts of information he was unable to share. 'You know how it is, I'm sure, being in the business of cutting out the opposition yourselves. Things are really on a 'need to know' only basis, at present.'

'That doesn't seem to include my mother, though, Tam,' David said.

'I just need to sort out some points with Mrs Logie about the gorge where her prize rhododendrons are. I thought it would be a courtesy.'

'That was thoughtful of you, Tam,' Agnes said. She smiled around the group and then added. 'If I can't be of any further assistance to you gentlemen, I might take Tam through to the snug.'

Agnes shook hands all round and, shortly, David was left with his prospective buyers. He guided them out to inspect the gardens and Rosalie returned to her pastry in a very thoughtful mood.

15

Wyn entered the kitchen and looked around. Rosalie could see she was shell shocked and must have overheard the discussion from the corridor. She couldn't think of anything to say that would lighten the moment for her.

'I'll just bring the trolley in, if that's okay?' Wyn said and disappeared back into the front hall. Within a couple of minutes, the service lift arrived in the kitchen and Wyn came back down the steps. She bustled about filling the dishwasher and still Rosalie could think of nothing sensible to say.

'I cannot imagine what's got into Tam Anscombe's head, Rosalie. Can you?' Wyn shut the dishwasher with some force and Rosalie had to catch the metal measuring jug she'd managed to dislodge from a shelf. 'He's just headed off down the front drive so the discussion with Mrs L didn't take very long, did it?'

'Well, possibly Betty hasn't said anything to you about a discussion we had with Mrs Logie last week.'

'Possibly she hasn't,' Wyn said in aggrieved tones. 'Being only the hired help around here . . . '

'Hey, Wyn, what's this?' Agnes asked as she stepped down into the kitchen. 'You're very much part of the team, but sometimes things work out better when fewer folk are in on them. You weren't in the kitchen while Tam was explaining his project, but if you had been you would have seen the surprise, if not astonishment on Rosalie's face.'

'Really?' Rosalie asked. 'I must admit I was taken by surprise. I know you've been down to see Tam once or twice, but I'd no notion it had got this far.' She took the cooked meat for the game pie out of the oven and set it on a counter.

'Just as well where you're concerned, too, my dear,' Agnes said. 'David did cast the odd look your way and you have such an honest face it's a good job what he was seeing was surprise.'

Rosalie reflected over this and concluded Agnes was right, but at the same time she had a sense of guilt because the threat of an unsavoury planning application hanging over the grounds had initially been her idea. The memory of David's quick hug and that tiny dropped kiss before the visitors arrived stirred feelings of regret and confusion.

She'd been impressed by the persistence Agnes had shown in following up the planning application idea. Either she really wanted to keep the house and its business ongoing, or she had a deeper belief that David simply needed time to work through his loss.

That thought caught Rosalie entirely unprepared. Was Agnes's publicly stated reason for resisting a sale born of a deeper need: the need to give David time to heal?

'Gracious, Rosalie, you look as if the proverbial has happened and someone has walked over your grave,' Agnes exclaimed.

'Not my grave,' Rosalie said.

'Ah!' Agnes replied.

* ★ ★

David banged the door of the carriage house behind him and dropped his documents onto the kitchen table. He went through to his big room and snapped on a light over the easel. The plans beginning to take shape there looked indistinct and sketchy.

'A bit like my life at the moment,' he said aloud.

He went back into the kitchen and lifted a bottle of Scotch from his drinks' shelf. He poured a largish measure and swirled the liquid around before drinking it down.

'Isn't it like medicine if you drink it like that?' Rosalie asked behind him.

'Has knocking before you barge in, gone out of fashion, then?' he snapped.

'Not exactly. You banged the door so hard, it bounced in the frame, I think.' She came up behind him and took the glass out of his hand. 'It was open.'

'Whose idea was that little scenario?' he asked, turning round so he could watch

Rosalie's reactions. 'You'll be unsurprised to hear that the firm are going to be in touch when they've checked out one or two other options they have in the area.' He loosened his tie with one hand and pulled it over his head. 'Whereas, before Tam came in and gave his performance, they thought their MD might like to make a personal visit over the weekend.' He dropped the tie onto the table and wrenched the top button of his shirt so hard, it flew off and pinged against a kitchen unit. 'Good result for the Remainers.'

'Tam's appearance was a surprise to me, too, David,' Rosalie said in a low voice. She kept her gaze firmly fixed on the whisky tumbler as she slid it further onto the table and David had the sensation that wasn't the whole truth. 'I just came across to ask whether you want dinner tonight. The note is out of date.'

David toyed with the idea of saying he'd rather eat in the pub, but was overwhelmed, suddenly and completely, by a sense of futility. He did not want to go into the village and meet people who'd heard about Tam's escapade. He could readily envisage the shoulders turning away as people became absorbed in the wallpaper pattern or anything that would help them avoid making eye contact. On the other hand, his mother would be only too keen to make eye contact and gloat.

'Mum feels her triumph won't be complete unless she gets the chance to rub it in?' He asked and heard just how petulant he sounded. All credit to Rosalie, he thought, as she let the childishness of his reaction slide over her without pointing it up.

'I don't think that's her viewpoint, but you know her better than me.' Rosalie let go of the glass and looked at him. 'I'm really sorry to have met you both when this battle is going on, but sometimes things aren't what they appear on the surface.'

'I suppose your recent experience with Steve allows you to say that,' David said. He nodded to the glass. 'I'm behaving like a toddler, sorry. Yes, I'd love some of that pie. The visitors really were salivating over it and even if they don't recommend the firm puts its money onto the purchase, I think you'll get a few bookings. They said there was an away day event coming up.'

'Good. Look I've been trying out a couple of desserts for the big wedding. I'd like some disinterested comments.' He saw the tiny smile playing around Rosalie's mouth and remembered what it had been like to kiss her. He fervently hoped the warmth he was feeling wasn't mirrored in a flush.

'Disinterested?'

'Your mum has a sweet tooth, I'd say, and would probably agree anything was good.'

'And I don't?'

'There is the genetic link, I suppose, but you are more inclined to tell it like it is . . .'

'Harsh,' he said, but grinned anyway. 'Trialling desserts. I wonder how I can get that onto my CV?'

'By becoming an hotelier,' Rosalie

said and turned on her heel.

David watched the slim figure walk purposefully across the kitchen and disappear into the yard. Was this appointment going to end well, he wondered. There was a core of strength in Rosalie Garden belied by her fragile figure and appearance.

16

Rosalie set the kitchen table and checked up on the pie which she now had cooking in the oven. David had sent a text to say he'd be over by seven-fifteen and Agnes was already downstairs.

The older woman had looked a little peaky when she came into the kitchen and was easily persuaded to put her feet up with the daily paper and a pre-dinner drink in the front sitting-room.

'Where's mother?' David asked. He'd come in while Rosalie was distracted by the meal and when she turned round she saw he was watching her from just inside the kitchen doorway. She noticed he'd brought Bracken in with him. He clicked his fingers and the dog trotted across to her favoured spot in front of the log-burning stove.

'That's a rather longing look she's sending over,' Rosalie said, and David turned back from the dog.

'No wonder. The kitchen smells amazing.' He smiled at Rosalie, and she felt her heart constrict. How she was going to miss all of this when her contract finished.

'Your mother is in the front sitting-room,' she said and felt sure the slight blush she saw cover David's cheeks was matched by one of her own. 'She was looking a bit hunted, so I took the daily paper and some sherry through to her.'

'I'll fetch her,' David moved across the room, 'If you're ready for us?'

'All done.'

While David collected his mother, Rosalie drained the vegetables and began to serve the food onto plates. Glancing out into the yard, she saw the shadow of a person cross the outer area beyond the carriage-house. The dogs raised an almighty din and Bracken leapt to her feet to take up guard behind the outer door. David and Agnes arrived then, and David raised a questioning eyebrow.

'Someone crossing the lawns. Dog walker maybe,' she said calmly.

'Poacher, lost tourist . . .' Agnes added, but sat down without joining David at the window. 'That does smell wonderful, my dear.'

'Thank you. I found some bags of game pieces in the freezer. Dougie must have laid them away for future use.' Rosalie wondered how long it could be before the afternoon visit was raised. She toyed with the idea of steering the conversation onto safe topics herself but decided it would only be postponing the inevitable.

'I suppose I shouldn't be surprised that Tam turns out to be a bit of an entrepreneur,' David said and sent his mother an enquiring glance. Rosalie saw the way she cocked her head and thought about it before replying.

'No, I suppose not. Although I think most of the business acumen is in Sadie's family. Her older brother runs a very successful garage across in Harrogate.'

'Right. So the dramatic talent displayed by Nancy is inherited from Tam, is it?' David asked with a broad grin.

Agnes was startled but simply shrugged. It would have been a mistake to start a discussion about Tam's supposed dramatic talents, so the older lady kept quiet.

* * *

Rosalie was in no doubt that David had checked out the council planning site after she left him earlier and discovered there was no application lodged. They finished their main course in silence, even if it wasn't quite companionable yet. Rosalie had high hopes for her new desserts. Maybe they would encourage mother and son to mellow a bit.

'I've made two puds,' she said as the others watched her take a bowl and a platter out of the fridge. 'I'm hoping to have your opinion on what to offer the wedding party. Curiously, the bride has left the choice up to us.'

Rosalie gestured towards Dougie's workbook. 'Dougie has noted that she said they weren't to be just strawberries but real puddings.'

'Just strawberries, eh? We get some of the most delicious strawberries in the world from our supplier in Angus,' Agnes said as she accepted the first real pudding to sample. 'What have you put in here, Rosalie. It smells fresh, minty.'

'Yes, there's mint and green apples, although they're not seasonal, but I see the young lady is decorating the ballroom with a lot of trailing greenery and I thought this would tie in.'

'What do you think?' Agnes looked across at David who had polished his off in no time.

'Couldn't possibly say till I've tried the other one.'

'Huh! You always had a sweet tooth. Although, I'd have to say, this is refreshing rather than sweet. Not a problem for me.' Agnes licked her spoon and smiled. Rosalie was relieved. She'd decided to take a risk on that one as it wasn't going to be a conventional wedding menu type offering.

'Okay, so clean spoons.' She pushed

three spoons round their places. 'This one is a cheesecake on a gingery biscuit base with a mix of dried fruits over. Dougie has noted the wedding cake will be chocolate sponge and not a fruit cake, so I thought this might make a good contrast.'

There was a longish silence which she took to be a good reception and quite soon David's plate was almost as clean as it had been before she put the pudding into it.

'Okay?' she asked at last.

'I might need to check that one out again,' David said with a raised eyebrow and slightly mischievous smile.

'I think not,' Agnes said and sent Rosalie an exasperated glance. 'If I didn't keep an eye on his sugar intake, he'd be as broad as a house.'

'Mum, I'm thirty, tripping over thirty-one. My waistline is no concern of yours.'

Rosalie cut a sliver of the cheesecake and slipped it onto David's plate, before adding a spoonful of the mint and apple compote to Agnes's. 'If you think they're up to standard, then I'd make both as an option,' she said, 'And I forgot to say, the compote will have a little shortbread biscuit, maybe with some fennel flavouring, on the side.'

'I suspect you'll have a riot, Rosalie,' David said in a semi-serious tone. 'Better make enough for at least the men to go back for seconds.'

'Oh, I don't want to upstage the baker,' Rosalie protested.

'I do,' Agnes contradicted her, 'And I'm fairly sure this cheesecake will do just that.'

While Rosalie and David cleared up, Agnes made herself a cup of herbal tea and headed off to her flat.

'What did this baker do?' Rosalie asked as soon as the kitchen door slid shut.

'I can't remember, but it was a major fight when it happened. Dougie threatening to resign. The brides bring their own cake of course, so she can't keep his stuff out of here.'

Rosalie made a mental note to ask Betty or Wyn for the story.

'I'm going to run the dogs as Bob is staying over at Aunty Bea's,' David said, 'Something to do with weed killer and second applications being needed first thing. Why don't you get out of the work stuff and join me?'

Rosalie thought about it for all of ten seconds. In fact, she realised she was nodding her assent as she stripped off her tunic and tossed it into the kitchen laundry bin.

'I'll join you in five,' she said and nipped up to her flat to pull a track-suit top on over her tee shirt and slide her feet into the trusty deck shoes. The midges should be in bed by now she thought but grabbed her roll-on insect repellent in case. No point in smelling quite so pharmaceutical unless it turned out to be needed.

* * *

David was standing beside the open kennels when she pulled the kitchen door behind her and turned the key. He was watching the dogs as they milled around waiting for him to choose a path.

'You look like an advert for Country House living,' she said.

'Flattery is a dangerous game to get started on, young lady. Where would you like to go?'

'Oh, don't you have a regular route for them?'

'I do, but I'm happy to vary it if there's a part of the grounds you'd like to see under this moon.'

They both gazed up at the nearly full moon hanging above them. It made the grounds eerily attractive.

'I haven't walked along the riverbank,' Rosalie said. 'It wanders through your woods for quite a distance.'

'We can do that. It'll be darker under the trees of course, but the path is level and Bob keeps it well maintained.' David called softly to Bracken and she set off around the walls of the kitchen garden with the small pack behind her. 'We just need to follow on.'

'Have the owners kept foxhounds?'

Rosalie cradled her powerful small torch in the pocket of her tracksuit top. Moonlight might be romantic, but it wasn't as illuminating as daylight by a long way and she thought the torch might get a lot of use before they returned.

'Not as far as I know,' David said. 'It's not foxhunting terrain around here, although that didn't always prevent owners from keeping the hounds and the horses, I'm sure.'

'I thought not. However, there's loads of small game. Does the house cater for shooting parties?' Rosalie hadn't seen any likely looking groups in Dougie's diaries, and she was a bit puzzled.

'Shooting parties?' David mused. 'No. My observation is that shooting parties need a leader and we haven't ever had a gamekeeper. My dad wasn't interested in field sports.'

'Are you?'

'No. I've done some clay-pigeon shooting and proved that the pheasants that stray onto the property are quite safe.'

'Ah,' she said and they both lapsed into silence. Rosalie was thinking about the startled bird they'd roused the first evening David took her out into the night. What, she wondered, is David thinking about?

'We don't keep any guns,' he said. 'The former gun room is full of wellies and long-forgotten jackets people have gone home without.'

'But someone fishes,' Rosalie said, 'Because there is a lot of river fish in the freezer at the back of the second garage.'

'That's me and Bob. We do rather well, but Mum doesn't think it should be fed to guests,' David said and laughed. 'She worries about the chain business you have to observe for food sourcing.'

'I can understand that, but I could use some of it for domestic dinners and personal guests, couldn't I?' Rosalie had seen a large pike among the stored fish and had been googling recipes for a couple of days. There was a particularly enticing French one called Brochet au Beurre Blanc.

'Rosalie,' David said on a sigh, 'You're making long-term plans and I really will sell.'

It was a blow, but she tried to deflect it. 'Of course, but I expect you'll still have the freezer and you can hire me freelance to come and cook dinner for your friends.'

David came to an abrupt stop and Rosalie banged into him.

'I don't think so,' he said quietly. 'I don't think I'd like that at all.' He moved off and Rosalie stood silenced, listening to the water gurgle in the river below the path.

17

Rosalie studied the list of names she'd been sent by the catering contractors who were going to help her with the upcoming wedding. She needed a couple of sous-chefs to assist on the day, in addition to the food the catering firm would be preparing off-site and bringing in.

'Morning, Rosalie,' Betty said as she arrived for her morning shift. 'I had a garbled phone call from Wyn last night about Tam delivering the performance of a lifetime.'

'Did you just?' Rosalie asked. 'It was quite something and the three young men from the investment management firm disappeared back to Newcastle pretty sharpish.'

'That's a result, then,' Betty said. She started to move towards the staffroom but stopped and said hesitantly, 'I went to the class.'

Rosalie held her breath. According to what David had hinted yesterday Betty getting to the class would be a bit of a result, too.

'And?' she asked.

'And, the man in charge was really nice. There were five other folk and two no-shows.' Betty shifted her bag from one arm to the other. 'If Mrs L agrees to a change in my shifts, I'd go again. There's a Tuesday class and one on Thursday — early evening.'

Rosalie got up and gave Betty a hug. 'Good for you.'

'Hey, what's this?' David asked from the doorway. 'Can anyone join in?'

'No,' Betty said firmly. 'You need to wait for the mistletoe at Christmas.' She winked at Rosalie and headed off to the staffroom.

'Is that an in-joke?' Rosalie asked.

'Could be,' David said. 'Actually, there was a year when the mistletoe in the barn was left up for about a month. We were all teens and, you know . . . ' He tailed off as if some memories were best left undisturbed. 'A list of names?' He nodded to the papers she had spread out.

'Yes, I asked the outside caterers for the names of promising sous-chefs. This is what they sent through. I recognise one or two of them so I'll make a choice, will I? Do I need to have anyone confirm it?' Rosalie asked.

'Nope. I wouldn't know a promising sous-chef as opposed to an unpromising one. You choose and let Mum have the names and financial details so they get paid.' He collected a cup of coffee and sat down at the table. 'Did Betty get to the class?'

'She did,' Rosalie said. 'And she's going to ask Agnes for a change in her shifts so she can go again.'

David drained his coffee. 'How did we manage before you arrived, chef? I need to head into Durham today. Do you want anything from the Cash & Carry?'

'There's a tidy little list actually. I spent some time making an inventory and now I know what I need to fill in the gaps.' Rosalie pulled the list out of her bundle of papers and wasn't at all surprised to see David's shoulders stiffen.

'Um! Why don't you come with me? Mum will give you the membership card and the business credit card. We could have a bite of lunch, too. There's a great little pub I know en route.' He put his empty cup in the dishwasher. 'Okay?'

'Well, yes,' Rosalie said while mentally adjusting what she'd serve for dinner that night. 'I'd like that.'

'Good. Depart at twelve. I'll get through some of the admin I've had piling up, meantime. Bracken!'

And they were gone. Rosalie felt the absence of the two of them perhaps more than she had their presence. Was this what it was like for David without Libby to come home to, she wondered.

* * *

Rosalie piled a couple of deep boxes and a bundle of hemp shoppers into the boot of the range rover which David had left open. She'd collected the store cards from Agnes and had them tucked securely into her shoulder bag.

'Ready?' David asked and she nodded in response.

'I haven't been north of Wolcester yet,' she said as they negotiated the haphazard parking in the centre of Maldington.

'I thought you said you'd spent a summer season on the Outer Hebrides?' David asked without making any big thing of it. Rosalie was pleased because it meant he was trusting her a bit more than he had been and not trying to catch her out in a lie.

'Well, yes, but I took the train across to Glasgow and then on as far as Oban. I have been north. I just meant, I've not explored the county around here,' she replied. 'Durham, on the other hand, I know quite well. Is most of your work conversions like the one you're doing for Bernie and Hamish?'

'It varies. The job in Durham is a new build but it's situated among existing buildings and on a difficult corner site. I keep having to go up to check out details,' David said. 'The devil is in the details.' He pulled out of their minor road onto the A class and Rosalie lapsed into silence.

She enjoyed watching the countryside flash past and relaxed more than she had done for months. There was a slight wobble in her composure as they passed the signs for Newcastle. She missed her dad and was even thinking she might like to see her mum, if she could avoid discussing Steve Baxter with her.

'Do you miss them?' David asked with that unexpected flash of empathy he sometimes showed.

'Mum and Dad? Yes, I think I do but I did work long hours, so I wasn't spending a lot of time with them,' she said. 'It's maybe the change in my circumstances. Now that I have a job and an income, I feel I could focus on them properly. Dad's mobility is a bit of an issue. I know he'll start off well with the physiotherapy, but he isn't the world's best at keeping on.'

'I hadn't noticed before,' David said as he pulled off the main road and took the car towards a village built into a hillside. Rosalie could see the sign for The Coach and Horses ahead. 'We're both the only children of rather elderly parents.'

'I suppose,' Rosalie said. 'Mum was forty-two when I was born and Dad's five years older.'

'My father was fifty-one when I came along. It makes the years you do have with them all the more precious. We're here, chef. A chance for you to try out someone else's cuisine.' David parked and they went into the pub through a glass atrium.

★ ★ ★

David watched Rosalie polish off the garlic mayonnaise on her plate with a scrap of bread she'd clearly kept back for the purpose.

'Those prawns didn't stand a chance,' he said and lifting a spare napkin from the centre of their little table, he leant across and wiped some of the sauce off the side of Rosalie's cheek. 'Do you always eat this fast?' He gestured to his half-finished burger. 'I've hardly begun.'

'Oh dear. Bad habit learned while needing to be ready to get started again,' Rosalie said. He loved the flush of colour he'd brought to her face. 'Split shifts are another bugbear. I can fall asleep anywhere, anytime.'

David smiled but at the same time he was a little concerned. Would Rosalie be returning to the hard grind of the restaurant world when her contract with them finished? He found he didn't much like the thought of that.

'What do you reckon to Mike's cooking then?'

'Surely there can't be anyone else you were at school with?' Rosalie asked with a giggle.

'Surely, there can. We haven't really scratched the surface yet. Mike, the chef-proprietor here, was actually in my cousin's class but we all kicked balls around together for years.' David signalled to a passing waitress.

'I thought my food was very good and

the smell of your burger was just right,' Rosalie said as they waited for the bill to arrive.

'The smell?' David was puzzled. 'You can tell how something will taste from its smell?'

Rosalie studied him silently and David wondered if he'd got stuff on his own face. There was plenty of melted cheese on top of his burger, maybe he'd got some of that stuck on his skin.

'Yes.'

David saw Mike Pritchard coming out of the kitchen and looking around the room. When Mike spotted them, he came across. His curiosity was so intense he virtually ignored David as he waited to be introduced.

'Been too long since you brought a young lady this way, man,' he said lifting Rosalie's hand from the table to kiss it flamboyantly.

'This is one of Mum's staff, Mike. She's called Rosalie Garden and she thinks your burgers smell good enough to eat.' David knew his description of her as staff had caused Rosalie to stiffen, but he had to ensure Mike didn't get the wrong idea. He hadn't brought anyone here for months and Mike was all too keen, along with everyone else he knew, to find him a significant other.

'Rosalie Garden, now why do I know your name, lovely lady?' Mike asked and, too late, David realised he might have avoided that or at least given Mike less of a clue.

'I was the owner of a business in Newcastle called . . .'

'Dinners at Your Leisure,' Mike interrupted. 'Knew I knew the name. May I say that your food smells good enough to eat, too.'

'Oh, did we do a dinner for you, Mr Pritchard?' she asked.

'Wife's thirtieth, Rosalie. I wanted the night off and the chance to relax.' Mike pulled out a spare chair and sat down. 'Tell me, do you own the recipe for the chestnut meringue we had that night?'

'I believe I do, but,' David could see Rosalie was struggling with the effects of thinking about her business.

'Mike, we need to be going. I've got an impatient client lined up . . . '

'When did you never? And what might the lovely Rosalie be spending her afternoon doing? I'd be more than delighted to act as sous if you wanted to recreate that chestnut meringue,' Mike said shamelessly and with no regard for the growing discomfort of his guests.

David decided he couldn't leave Rosalie here to be badgered about recipes she clearly thought might be tangled up in some legal process or other.

'Mike, give it a rest.'

'What? Oh, if you insist.' He waved the waitress away. 'Mr Logie is my guest.' Much to David's irritation, Mike walked them to their car where he spotted the pile of shoppers in the back.

'Are you making this woman spend her afternoon at the Cash & Carry? Honestly, David, anybody would be forgiven for thinking you had no intention of getting married again.'

Anger bubbled through David. 'Mike,

do you remember we had a big fight just as you were leaving school?'

'What? Did I speak out of turn?' Mike affected to be genuinely puzzled as he turned to Rosalie. 'He's got that beautiful house, you know.'

'I'm trying to sell the main house. The carriage house is big enough for my needs,' David protested as his exasperation got the better of him.

'I think his brain is in need of rest, lovely lady.' Mike turned to David then. 'I do remember our fight. We said it was over some girl or other, but in fact it was because I referred to your dad as a dithering, true-blue, landed twit.'

'Ever the gentleman, eh Mike? And now you criticise me for attempting to divest myself of said house and land.'

'I was eighteen, very drunk and furious that you had a place in life mapped out for you whereas I had to go it alone. And your dad was a very nice man, if a bit posh.' Mike shrugged and kissing Rosalie on both cheeks, banging David on the back and patting the front of the range rover, he headed back to his kitchen.

'Rosalie, I'm sorry about that. It was meant to be a pleasant break for you,' David apologised.

'The food was great, and I can cope with the occasional reminder of what my cooking was like.' She climbed into the passenger seat.

'Was? The smells around the house when you're cooking are fabulous.'

'Thanks, but I mean when people hired me to do something very special for them.'

'I see,' David said. He supposed it wasn't quite the same being at one remove behind Agnes. 'Mike knew from an early stage that he was going to be a chef. I think he did resent the fact that I had a readymade venue and no clear idea of what could be done with it,' David said by way of explanation.

Rosalie simply nodded.

18

Payday came round at last. Rosalie went online from the chef's laptop in the kitchen. Everyone else was otherwise occupied so she had a few private moments to deal with transferring funds to the family's legal firm. They'd waited long enough, and her parents had supported her so strongly while they waited. She studied the up-to-date statement of her new account.

Completely unprepared for the force of the emotion that coursed through her, she felt a tear escape and brushed it away impatiently from her cheek. This moment was the one she'd been working towards since the horrible day the bailiffs padlocked shut her business premises.

'Get a grip, Rosalie, why don't you? A row of black numbers over 100 will happen every month you earn money.' She pulled her document wallet of papers across the table and was just taking out copies of the lawyers' most recent demand when the phone rang.

'Hullo Chef,' Steve said in her ear, 'Just wanted to be sure you were there before popping in.'

She said nothing. What was the point?

'Don't try the silent treatment on me, lover. I know you'll have been paid and I'm calling by to make sure you keep some of the money back for me.' Rosalie was startled by the venom in Steve's tone. What right did he have to stake any claim to her salary? Still she held her peace.

'Listen up, Rosalie Garden, if you don't make my life a bit easier than it is at present, I'll make yours a lot more unpleasant. Damn! Where did he come from?'

Rosalie realised the line had gone dead. She was almost sure Steve was driving and, also, that his voice sounded slurred. No matter, she thought, this is my moment. Quickly she entered the details into the transfer document on screen. She double-checked them and sent the payment through.

The statement of her account would be so much less next time she looked, but still in the black with enough to pay her phone contract and allow her to go back to Newcastle on the train. She picked up her mobile and rang her dad's.

'Dad, I've paid the lawyers,' she blurted out. 'I've started to repay my debt to you and Mum.'

'Rosalie, lass, you shouldn't have done that. We're managing, you know.'

'I know, but I also know you shouldn't have to 'manage'. You should be enjoying retirement after all the years of hard work.' She realised she was going to cry and quickly cut off the call. 'Sorry, Dad, Mrs L's looking for me. I'll phone again later.'

Rosalie headed for the back door and unbolted it. Bracken was at her heels and together they went out to the pond along the little path. Once there Rosalie let her feelings go and wept as she hadn't since she was a small child. Bracken huddled around her legs and brushed against her

243

in a way Rosalie found comforting. The debt was diminishing.

★ ★ ★

In the following days, Rosalie worked very hard on the planning for the big wedding and there were a few small parties of guests coming through as well. Betty and Wyn turned to, like the loyal workers they were, and Mandy Doig arrived to help with changeover days. Marcus had been cast in an advert shoot and was down in London for a week.

'It's not as if I couldn't do the part just as well as him, but the client said they needed an authentic male swagger,' Mandy grumbled as she stashed breakfasting food away in the kitchen. 'Those girls can eat,' she added dramatically, 'This cereal packet is empty.' She turned it upside down for emphasis and covered the floor in a fine dusting of cereal crumbs.

'What is an authentic male swagger?' Rosalie asked. She watched in amusement as Mandy cast her a withering glance, threw back her head and swaggered across the kitchen to bump into David as he came in.

'Rehearsing, Mandy?' he asked. Rosalie watched with concern as he rubbed his shin, but Mandy was oblivious to any damage she might have caused.

'No. Demonstrating to Rosalie why the client could have had me for his advert instead of my male brother. I can swagger every bit as well as Marcus.' Mandy headed out into the yard and they heard her sweet-talking Bracken who spent most days stretched across the kitchen entrance as she wasn't allowed in when there were guests living in the house.

'In my experience brothers are likely, or always, male,' David said sending Rosalie a grin.

'Indeed,' she said. 'Are they never apart? Mandy seems a little diminished without him.'

'What an interesting remark. I think you're right. She does seem a little subdued,' David mused. He jingled his car keys. 'I'm off up to Highmere for most of the day and I wanted to ask whether your salary came through without any issues. If there's a problem, I could go into the bank on my way.' David spoke diffidently and Rosalie sent him a reassuring smile. She'd got over the embarrassment she felt when he made her the advance payment and was glad to have him check up on the system.

'Thanks, yes. I went online and attended to some business yesterday.' She smiled again. 'It's a good feeling to be back in the black and I am grateful to you and Agnes for taking a chance on me.'

David blushed. 'Good, well, I'll be off. I won't get back in time for dinner, I'm afraid.'

The unspoken question hung in the air between them. Where was Steve and why had none of them seen him in recent days? Their egg delivery had been left in the yard. Rosalie could hardly complain because she knew she'd screamed at Steve to do just that early on.

She met David's concerned gaze and shrugged. 'I don't know,' she said. 'He was briefly in touch, but sounded drunk, I'm sorry to say.'

'Are you two going in for psychic communication or what?' Mandy asked from the doorway. 'No, Bracken. Not today.' She pushed the setter back out onto her blanket.

'Maybe,' David said and grinned broadly, 'Maybe we're tuning into the vibe you and Marcus use.'

'No way. It's blocked by the London traffic in any case,' Mandy said. 'If the unspoken was about Steve Baxter, I can tell you something.'

Rosalie stiffened. Even allowing for Mandy's irrepressible dramatizing, there was an air of gossipy scandal about her tone.

'And that would be?' David asked. Rosalie wasn't brave enough.

'He was pulled over by the traffic police two days ago. Came in under the limit when breathalysed, but they chewed his ear off.' Mandy headed towards the steps out of the kitchen. 'I hear LayBright Eggs aren't too impressed.'

David studied the space where Mandy had stood, and Rosalie saw the conflicting emotions chase across his face.

'If Steve loses his job, he'll have to go back to Newcastle, won't he?' David said.

Steve would have to leave if he no longer had a job in the area. Would he, she wondered. Wouldn't he simply persuade his long-suffering cousin that it was a blip and he'd find something else and stay off the booze again? She met David's unblinking stare.

'I don't know, David. He can be remarkably tenacious.' She shrugged.

'Don't you care, woman?'

'Care? What about? I didn't ask Steve to follow me here. In fact, I went to a lot of trouble to prevent him discovering where I was . . .'

'I'm sorry. That was unforgivable of me.'

Rosalie didn't reply and after a few seconds, David turned on his heel and left the kitchen. Bracken whimpered as he left her behind. Rosalie went out to the dog and stroked her ears.

'I know how you feel, girl,' she said.

* * *

Relations with David remained tense as the week of Rosalie's first big wedding arrived.

'Thank goodness David will be off-site when we have the wedding reception in full swing,' Agnes said at breakfast on the Thursday. 'I really do not believe I could cope with his fixed smile and tense jaw-line greeting the guests.'

Rosalie dipped her head in confusion over the chicken dish she was cooking for the families of the bride and groom who would be arriving the next day. She could only agree. David's detachment had been difficult to deal with and she was acutely aware that his unhappiness was making her unhappy, too.

'The two sous-chefs are arriving in Wolcester at eleven,' she said by way of distraction. 'Any chance someone could collect them from the station?'

'Of course, my dear, it's in the diary. I think Wyn's going.' Agnes cocked her head. 'That sounds like the marquee lorry arriving so Bob will be busy with them for the rest of the day.'

'By the way, Agnes, why won't David be here on Saturday?'

'He's arranged a site visit in Durham over that new house he's designing,' Agnes replied before taking a deep breath and continuing, 'But if what you're asking has a different question behind it, then I think he simply finds it too hard, still, to be here where he and Libby entertained their guests in a marquee,' Agnes replied.

Rosalie thought about that for a moment or two. 'Yes,' she said quietly, 'That would be very hard, still.'

* * *

The day of the wedding arrived in a pre-dawn shower of fine rain that freshened all the shrubbery and dried off in the

250

midsummer sun. Rosalie was up early. With Bracken at her heels, she jogged round the perimeter of the kitchen garden until she felt her muscles loosen and her head clear of the jumbled chaos of menus and timings that had been clogging her brain for the best part of a week. By six-thirty, she had breakfast for the two families well underway and ancillary people were beginning to arrive.

The photographers came first but they were closely followed by a make-up artist and a hairdresser. Everyone moved around calmly and she was pleasantly surprised by the absence of hysteria.

'Have you done a wedding before?' Mandy Doig asked as she and Marcus came in through the back entrance.

'Yes, but it was that slightly quirky one for nine,' Rosalie said. She and Keith had cleared off breakfast and he was deep in prepping vegetables. 'I must say, the caterers are cutting it a little fine.' She nodded to the wall-clock.

'You're right,' Marcus said. 'Usually that firm are very reliable, though, so don't panic yet.'

'I saw their minibus in the village,' Mandy added, 'The one that brings their waiting staff. The refrigerated van was parked there, too.'

'Good, it has the first course in it,' Rosalie said.

She began to relax again. If the waiting staff and the first course were in the village, then surely the other transport with her two sous chefs and the firm's function manager wouldn't be far behind.

The back door opened again, and a large, rather florid gentleman came into the kitchen. He was staggering under the weight of the huge box in his arms.

'Is that the cake?' Rosalie asked.

'Certainly, it is. Where do you want it? Where's the chef?' The man made it to the large table in the centre of the kitchen and set the box onto it.

'The chef?' he repeated rudely, 'Are you deaf, girl?'

'I'm the chef,' Rosalie said, and a calmness settled in her. How dare he, she wondered.

'She's reduced to hiring lasses to do a man's job is she?'

Rosalie felt Keith's anger wash over her in a wave and she could see Marcus's fingers turning white as he gripped the apron strings he was tying around his waist. David came into the kitchen at that moment and while she knew he'd heard the baker's gibe, she realised in an instant that something else was worrying him. The lines around his eyes were deeply defined and his face was almost grey.

While the baker drummed his fingers on the table, Rosalie crossed over and threw back the lid of the box. The cake inside looked fabulous and she could understand why their bride had chosen it. However, she didn't think for a moment that this insufferable man should be allowed to swan in here and undermine her authority.

'I believe the order was for a chocolate cake,' she said evenly.

'And what does that look like?'

'It looks chocolate covered,' Rosalie

said, 'But it does not smell like a confectionery product made from 70% quality chocolate.' She lifted her head and stared at the baker. He began to quiver around the jaw and a nasty dark flush crept slowly up his throat. Rosalie had a momentary twinge of guilt. How would she feel if the man had a heart attack, she wondered.

Agnes came into the kitchen from the main house.

'Mrs Logie,' the baker said, 'This cake is the chocolate cake ordered by the bride you're hosting today. If I may say so . . .'

'I don't advise you to say anything else,' David interrupted. 'If Chef Garden thinks you've skimped on the chocolate, she's likely to be correct. Her nose for flavour is widely recognised in the business.'

'Thank you, David. If you've brought your goods, Sherriff, I'd ask you to leave. We're busy,' Agnes said and turned to Keith. 'Can you have this moved into the servery, please, Keith?'

Mr Sherriff opened his mouth, but in the face of so much hostility, decided he didn't have anything else to say and turning about, left the house.

'I did mean to ask Betty about him,' Rosalie said, 'Now, I don't need to.'

'Rosalie,' David said so quietly she strained to hear him. 'There's been an accident. The third vehicle coming from the caterers was struck side-on by a tractor. Both the sous chefs and the function manager have been taken to hospital.'

Rosalie felt the blood drain from her and reached behind to find a chair. Mandy jumped and caught her as she swayed.

'Marcus!'

Together the twins lowered her onto an upright kitchen chair. David meantime went around and settled his mother in another one on the other side of the table.

As the room came back into focus, Rosalie asked quietly, 'How badly injured are they?'

'I didn't get much. It was Mike

Pritchard who phoned as he was driving behind them, and he saw the logo on the car. He thinks maybe a few broken bones. Possibly concussion.'

'Thank goodness,' Agnes said. 'It was a mistake not to put the chefs up here.'

'Good to know they're not badly hurt,' Rosalie murmured. Her head was spinning again as she began to re-allocate jobs across the crew she did have. Could they manage?

19

'Rosalie,' David said, and she focussed on his eyes. Why hadn't she noticed before that they had a speckled appearance, she wondered. 'I've cancelled my trip to Durham.'

'Really? Why?'

'Because you'll need all the help you can get, however unskilled,' David said impatiently. 'It'll be like having a really good kitchen porter who's almost a sous chef,' he nodded towards Keith who was wrestling the wedding cake box onto a trolley, 'And a really inept kitchen porter who's not even a KP.'

'And a sous chef who's not very good at taking orders, but who'll try,' Mike Pritchard said from just inside the kitchen door. 'So, Chef, where should I start?'

'Mike,' David said, 'What're you doing here? What about your restaurant?'

'It's a pub, and my own team are out

in force. They'll manage. I couldn't leave your lovely young lady here to sink, now could I?' He stripped off the jacket he was wearing, and Marcus leapt into action to find tunics for both David and Mike from the staff linen cupboard.

'Mike,' Agnes said in a rather faint voice that caused Rosalie to glance over at her, 'This is very good of you. It's been several years since we saw you here.'

'You know what life's like when you're in the catering trade, Mrs Logie,' Mike said. 'Angie sends her love, by the way.'

'Thank you, Mike,' Rosalie said, 'And you, David. Now, if the twins could head out to the dining-room where the drinks reception will be, and the cake is to be cut before everyone moves to the marquee for the meal, that would reduce the congestion in here. Agnes, maybe you'd like to rendezvous with the head waiter, please. I think he's called Raul. He's probably heard about the accident, but as he'll have to take on the duties of function manager, if you were at his side, it would help to smooth his way.'

People headed off to their various tasks and Rosalie was left in the kitchen with the three men. Keith spoke first.

'I'll get this monstrosity up to the servery, Chef, and then I'll be back. David,' he nodded towards the sink where he'd been working before Sherriff came barging in, 'I'm just starting on the mange tout.'

'Got it,' David said, 'I know a pea when I see fifteen trays of them . . . '

'There are one hundred and fifty guests,' Rosalie said. 'Mike, there are forty vegetarian options. Could you take that in hand, please?'

'Certainly, Chef.' He was holding one of the menu cards. 'Looks scrumptious, I do say. So, how do I stuff a cabbage?'

Bob chose that moment to open the back door. 'Morning everyone. Hullo, Mike. What're you doing here?'

'Filling in. How's it going, Bob?'

'Okay, okay,' Bob said absently, 'Rosalie, we heard about the accident. Betty has phoned her sister, Em, and she's getting her man to drive her over. She does a bit of silver service waiting at a big hotel in Newcastle. If you like, she can join the caterers' team in the marquee. That's supposing they're all stepping up.'

'Bob, that's good. Has the wine team arrived?' Rosalie mentally ticked off another gap and smiled gratefully at the gardener.

'I've just got them parked up. I'll get back to it. Betty and Wyn are supporting Mrs L and they'll keep an eye on the facilities as they usually do.'

★ ★ ★

David bent to his task and soon had a bigger pile of mange tout on the prepped side of his station than on the waiting side. His pulse had been thumping when he arrived in the kitchen and when he heard that buffoon Sherriff, he felt it ratchet up to a level he hadn't ever experienced. The quiet repetition of the work in the vegetable sink was soothing.

I feel, he thought with some surprise, as if my brain has gone into neutral after too many years of hurrying on to reach the next goal, straddle the next hurdle. Behind him in the kitchen, Rosalie and Mike were moving around exchanging questions and answers in a calm and professional manner. She'd risen to the challenge in the best way possible by simply accepting the help people had offered. There'd been no histrionics, no raised voices, although he could see how hard she was working to sort out a plan before Mike arrived.

'Great, David, will you finish them if I start on the dishwashers?' Keith asked at his back, startling him out of his reverie.

'Can do,' David said. 'Though, shouldn't I be doing that and handing the food over to you?'

Rosalie appeared at his side. 'The mange tout look good to me,' she said, 'And Keith loves arranging the dishwashers. I might have to marry him to allow full rein to his OCD where stacking plates is concerned.'

'Thanks, Chef, I'm spoken for,' Keith said as he set a tray of breakfast crockery down.

'Really?' David asked. 'Did we know that? Has Mary agreed?'

'She will,' Keith said, 'Particularly when I tell her there's another woman waiting in the wings.'

Typical Keith, David thought as Betty's sister, Em, burst in on them from the yard. Mary didn't stand a chance.

'Good morning, Chef,' the newcomer said to Rosalie, and David mentally hugged her. And Betty, who'd no doubt impressed on her what was what. 'I see the marquee, but thought I'd just touch base first. Do you need me?'

'We definitely need you, Em,' Rosalie said and shook hands. 'The head waiter is Raul and he's probably been asked to step up to function manager. Mrs Logie is across there giving him a hand.'

'I'm on my way. Morning, Mike. How's Angie and the boys?' Em asked cheerily with one hand on the outer door.

'Doing well, thanks, Em. And you?' Mike answered without raising his head from the enormous pile of asparagus he was working his way through with a sharp knife.

David screened out the rest of their conversation as he finished prepping the peas.

How lucky was his mother that she'd sent him to the local schools? This was her reward as the community rallied around to save her, and the bride's, day.

*　*　*

Rosalie's brain was in full action mode as she moved through her own tasks and those of the missing sous chefs. Having Mike Pritchard at her back was a bonus from Heaven and she sent a silent prayer of thanks winging up to whichever Saint dealt with catering. Before he walked into her kitchen, she'd been scaling back the accompanying vegetables, reducing the two puds to one and wondering whether the entertainer the family had hired for that gap when the bride and groom are being endlessly photographed, could do another round between the first course brought down from Newcastle by the catering firm, and the mains.

It was still going to be tough, but they should get everything out on time and as described in the menu. And David? She sneaked a quick glance across to the dessert station where he was now measuring double cream into one of the big bowls ready to whisk it. The grey pallor had brightened considerably, and she'd been fascinated by the way his tight shoulders had relaxed as he worked over the peas earlier.

Hours passed in a tightly managed blur of activity until that moment when the happy, slightly drunk, assembled guests wanted to applaud the chef. Rosalie was used to appearing briefly in people's dining-rooms where maybe twenty were crammed around a large table. The idea of taking a bow in front of one hundred and fifty with the band playing a drum roll, was overwhelming.

'I can't do that,' she said as Agnes asked her.

'Take Mike.'

'No,' Mike said firmly. 'Forever after, there would be arguments about who the real chef was and I didn't create this triumph, lovely lady — you did. Besides, I need to get back to base and see how my own squad are doing.' He leant across the table where they were having a welcome coffee and kissed Rosalie on both cheeks. 'It's been a revelation and a huge pleasure.'

He was out of the kitchen then and the others were left looking at each other.

'That's Mike,' Keith said. 'He just didn't fancy doing the bacon rolls for the evening guests coming in at eleven.'

'Could be,' David agreed, 'But we can't hold that against him.' He came round behind Rosalie's chair and eased her out of it. 'Come along, Chef. The sooner you do this, the sooner it's over.'

Rosalie stiffened as David's hands cupped her elbows and lifted her upwards. She battled a rising wave of panic as he tucked her right hand through his arm and drew her to the back door.

'David, really, I cannot do this.' She

was aware of Keith and Agnes waiting and of the music pulsing across the lawns from the marquee.

'I'll be with you,' David said, 'Although I'm removing this chef's tunic just in case the punters get the wrong idea. And Mum will be there, too.'

Agnes moved then, and as she began to walk, Rosalie fell into step beside her. She couldn't remember later how she'd felt as the lights in the marquee dimmed and then flared and the irrepressible MC had brought her forward to take a bow in front of the assembled wedding party. She did remember her total shock over a question from one of the wedding guests.

They'd been easing their way back out of the huge tent when a man stopped David to shake hands.

'Great to see how this all works on the ground, David. I understand the house is for sale and I'll be in touch next week,' he said with a serious expression. 'So often 'attractive businesses' are anything but. Your mother has built this up beautifully.' He turned to Rosalie and added,

'And we'll be looking to keep on as many of the staff as possible.'

Rosalie had nodded dumbly and escaped to the kitchen where several dozen bacon rolls needed attention.

20

David didn't return to the kitchen but sent the Doig twins to assist with the evening supper buffet. He steered his mother into the house by the little used front door and up the enclosed stair to her flat where he advised her firmly to stay put as she was exhausted. He felt a little guilty about Rosalie because he was fairly sure she'd been up and out with Bracken early but following the unexpected offer just made to him about the house, he had things to attend to which wouldn't wait.

It was hardly seven the following morning when he turned the range rover off the main road and along an ever-narrowing farm access to Highcroft. Rick and Hazel Easton were already out in the yard attending to their livestock when David pulled in.

'David,' Rick said. 'What brings you here, man?' He glanced along one of the tracks to a gaggle of rickety shed type buildings. Those must be his bothies, David thought, and he already knows I'm looking for Steve Baxter.

'I'd like a word with your cousin,' he said. The furrows in Rick's forehead deepened to a frown and David wondered what else could have happened since the incident Mandy told them all about.

'Oh aye. You and the local constabulary, both. He's not here,' Rick said bluntly.

'Was he arrested?'

'What makes you ask that?'

'One of Mum's staff picked up the idea he'd been pulled over by the traffic police. She did think he'd been under the limit but got an earful of advice.'

'That was true. However, he got into a bit of a fight yesterday morning and by midday my uncle and aunt had arrived here,' Rick sighed in exasperation.

'His parents? How do they fit in to all of this? He's in his thirties.' David couldn't imagine getting into a random fight but if he did, he sure as hell wasn't going to phone Agnes to get him out of trouble. One of his older cousins, maybe, but not his mother.

'Aye, but they paid for him to do a rehab stint when everything went pear-shaped with his drinking. Apparently, it's not uncommon for folk to need more than one shot at that kind of thing. They've agreed to fund another go and they carried him off.'

Hazel had been listening to all this and rubbed a hand supportively down her husband's arm. 'He thought the police would be impressed if he was back in rehab. I'm not sorry to see him go, David. He's a difficult and troubled man,' she said. 'Rick offered him the bothy and put in a good word for him at LayBright Eggs, but he's been back on the drink.'

'Aye, and garbling,' Rick said. 'Told Tam Anscombe that nice chef your mother took on, stole a family heirloom worth thousands of pounds.'

'Did he now?' David said.

'He says she pawned it.'

'As if,' Hazel said, 'Anybody can see she's as honest as anything whereas he's not.'

'Would it be too much trouble for you to give me your uncle's telephone number, Rick?' David asked diffidently. 'There's a couple of issues surrounding Rosalie's break-up with Steve that need attention.'

'Aye, no doubt,' Rick said and added, 'You'll be acting on your mother's behalf.'

While David didn't actually agree with Rick's assessment, he made an undefined movement of his head and took a moleskin notebook out of his pocket ready to write down the details.

★ ★ ★

Rosalie was up and about by half-past six and heard David's big car driving out of the yard. She opened the kitchen door in time to see it disappear and to welcome Bracken across to her mat.

'Clever girl,' she soothed the dog, 'I

271

suppose he's gone to catch up on the work he missed out on yesterday.' She heard people moving in the kitchen behind her and when she turned round found Agnes studying her with a quizzical expression.

'Do you expect that dog to answer?' Agnes asked.

Rosalie laughed. 'Good morning. I see the team is up.' Both the Doigs were slumped at the kitchen table, Keith was distributing orange juice and Wyn was pouring water into the coffee machine. They had gone off to their respective homes the previous night, but Bob had been round the area to pick everyone up.

'Last push, Chef,' Mandy said. 'Breakfast for seventeen.'

'But not until there's been breakfast for six here first,' Marcus added. 'I need coffee.'

'Where're Bob and Betty?' Rosalie asked.

'They like to have theirs in the cottage,' Agnes said. 'It went brilliantly, Rosalie. I am so sorry I disappeared after the meal.'

'Don't worry about that at all. I could see you were out on your feet.'

Marcus pushed himself up from his chair and lifting his glass of orange juice said, 'I propose a toast to Chef Garden. Long may she reign.'

The others leapt up and joined in till Rosalie was covered in confusion and protesting.

'I couldn't have done it without you all and David and Mike were brilliant, too.' The thought made her a little reflective. David had seemed to throw himself into the emergency and thrive on it.

'David,' Agnes said, 'He did surprise me.'

'Surprised me more that he didn't hang about for a bacon roll,' Keith said as he slotted bread into the toaster. 'He hardly ate a thing throughout the day.' He waved Rosalie away when she headed for the fridge. 'Sit down, Chef. You'll have enough on your hands in,' he looked at the wall-clock, 'Twenty-three minutes. Enjoy being waited on till then.'

Rosalie did as she was told. It gave

her a few moments grace to puzzle over David's disappearance last night and his early departure this morning. She had thought he'd enjoyed seeing how the house functioned as a wedding venue and she dared to hope he'd got over his distress at seeing a marquee in the same place as it had been for his own marriage. Something seemed to loosen in him as he worked at the various stations she'd given him.

On the other hand, his withdrawal from the wedding came immediately after the offer his acquaintance had made about buying the business. Rosalie looked over at Agnes. The older woman was very tired this morning although the triumph they'd pulled from a near-disaster yesterday was clearly buoying her up, too.

Agnes, as if aware of Rosalie's regard, raised her head. 'I'm wondering if I'm getting too long in the tooth for big wedding receptions,' she said.

'Maybe,' Rosalie agreed, 'But maybe the shock of the accident knocked you more off balance than you gave it credit.'

'Maybe it did. There were several e-mails this morning from the caterers. The youngsters who were in the accident have all been discharged,' Agnes said.

'That must be good, Mrs L,' Wyn said as she put yogurt and fruit on the table. 'They'd have been kept in otherwise, wouldn't they?'

'I suppose,' Agnes agreed. 'Their managing director is coming to see us tomorrow. He heard how we managed to cobble a team together and all without alerting the clients there was anything going on behind the scenes.'

Hearing their work summed up like that made Rosalie conscious of what they'd achieved. It was, she thought at last, remarkable.

Sadly, the success of the wedding was going to be the nail in their hopes of suppressing the house sale. David's business acquaintance had been impressed: impressed enough to be seeking a visit later in the week. Rosalie was conflicted. Continuing here as chef would enable her to go on living cheaply and re-paying her father. On the other hand, it would be very hard to go on living so close to David Logie. In that moment, she knew she couldn't.

Rosalie realised she'd fallen in love with David. There was no possibility of continuing here when he didn't return her feelings.

* * *

On Tuesday, Rosalie drove Betty into Wolcester for her reading group. They'd left Agnes getting ready to go out to a bridge evening with Alastair Craig.

'Do you think Alastair Craig will ever get round to popping the question?' Rosalie asked Betty.

'Naw,' Betty said on a long, expelled breath. 'Naw, he would've done it three years ago when his mother died, if he'd wanted. I think they get along just fine.'

'He squires her around, you mean?' Rosalie asked.

'That's the expression David uses. Did

you hear him say it?' Betty laughed a little as she gathered her papers together.
Rosalie could see they were worksheets
and that on most of them Betty had
made an attempt at least to complete
some of the exercises set.

'No. I haven't heard David say very
much about the man. That is apart from
his harping on about turning the house
into a spa.'

Betty raised her eyebrows dismissively.

'He won't do that either. Funny how
you can tell. Mr Craig is a nice man and
he does have ideas, but he doesn't ever
act on them. I think that's why he won't
marry Mrs L. It suits him really well the
way things are at present.' Betty sat on
even though they were just on time for
the class and Rosalie thought she might
be a little nervous.

'I see, whereas, David and Agnes
are both people who get on and do it.
Maybe Agnes will ask him,' Rosalie said
cheerfully. She wondered whether there
was any chance she'd ask David and dis-
missed the idea out of hand.

'I think she'd really like to see David marry again,' Betty said quietly, 'And give her some grandchildren.'

'He is still young enough for all of that,' Rosalie said. 'Betty, would you like me to come in with you?'

'No, well yes, but no. I've got to do this. Bob is picking me up on his way back from Aunty Bea's.' Betty opened the car door and slid out onto the pavement. 'Thanks for the lift, Chef.'

Rosalie drove back to the house and saw the range rover sitting in the yard as she turned in. David was in the kitchen and Bracken came bounding over from her place in front of the log stove.

'Didn't take her long to winkle her way back in after the wedding guests left,' David said cheerily. 'What's for dinner? I'd like to open a bottle of wine.'

Momentarily taken aback, Rosalie had to think. What was for dinner? Leftovers probably, she thought.

'Your mum has gone out with Alastair. We could tackle some of the wedding leftovers. There were some of the lamb shanks spare and a few of the vegetarian option.' Rosalie said.

'Was that really stuffed cabbage?'

'No, Mike was acting up. It was a savoury baklava', she protested.

'Hmn, I quite fancy some of that, please. If it doesn't make any difference to forward plans,' David replied. He disappeared down to the wine cellar.

Rosalie took dishes out of the fridges and set the oven to come on automatically. It was barely five-thirty and a little earlier than they were used to eating.

David came back carrying a bottle of red wine. 'My father laid this down. I think we deserve something a little special after the wonderful effort at the weekend.'

'You were an enormous help, thank you. I hope you found your client was okay about the changed plans when you went over on Sunday morning,' Rosalie said and was astonished to see the red blush that fired David's cheeks. Perhaps he hadn't been to Durham, then. Perhaps he'd been to see the man who expressed an interest in buying the house.

'The Durham site is doing fine, Rosalie,' he said at last. 'I was using it as an excuse to be off this place when the wedding was going ahead.'

'It must be very hard . . .'

'It was very hard,' he interrupted, 'For a long time it was genuinely very hard. When I picked up Mike's call about the accident, though, that wasn't my first thought.'

'No, you'd be worried about the young people, as we all were,' Rosalie said remembering how her legs had given way beneath her and Mandy had to catch her.

David sent her an assessing glance that made her wonder if her hair had fallen down or she had tomato sauce on her nose. He raked a bit in a drawer and found a corkscrew. She watched him set the sharp point into the top of the bottle's cork and screw the shaft down. Within a minute, there was a satisfying pop as the cork left the bottle.

David held the open bottle below his

nose and inhaled. 'Very promising,' he said. He squinted into the oven Rosalie had set.

'I've opened the wine to breathe and I see you've put some dishes into the oven on automatic we could take a walk.' He strode across the room and opened the door onto the yard. Rosalie felt the afternoon breeze ripple over her and drew in a lungful of herby, newly-cut grass smell.

'Bob must have been cutting the lawns again,' she said. Did she want to go wandering in the grounds with David now that she'd decided not to stay on after the house changed hands?

As if he sensed her indecision, David took her by the elbow and guided her across the yard onto the path to the pond. She didn't resist and Bracken loped ahead. The summer afternoon enfolded them.

21

They reached the pond and David guided her round its edge until they came to another path which was almost overgrown by a pair of viburnums. David pushed the branches apart and they were able to get through.

'Where are we going?' Rosalie asked.

'You'll see. A couple more minutes,' he said and heard her indrawn breath as a tiny summerhouse came into view. He wondered what the interior would be like, but it didn't matter. He simply wanted a private space away from the phone and all of the staff who dropped by when the fancy took them.

They pushed the door inwards and David was surprised it didn't smell as dank and unused as he'd expected.

'I wonder if Mum has been coming here,' he said. He reached into his pocket and brought out his flashlight. 'Yep. She always liked it, but I thought after Libby died, she'd given up on it. Maybe not.'

He watched Rosalie scan the little room and take in the basket chairs, the small table with its glass top and a basket-weave shelf underneath and the group of swallows' nests in the corner. The furniture wasn't in pristine condition, but it wasn't festooned in cobwebs either.

They sank into a chair each. He switched the torch off and there was just enough natural light seeping through the overgrown shrubs outside to allow them to see each other. Above them, the birds twittered in the nests. Rosalie glanced up briefly before turning her attention to him. David knew she'd be puzzled.

'I've spent the last couple of days chasing after Steve,' he said baldly.

'What? Why?'

'Don't panic, please. I didn't get to talk to him because he's back in rehab and the staff felt it wouldn't be in his interests to have any contact with someone from his 'failed' attempt to stay sober,' David said. He wished he didn't have to visit this pain on Rosalie, but he hoped the rest of what he had to say was going to be better for her to hear.

'I got his parents' contact details from Rick Easton. I must say, Hazel was glad to see him go,' David said. 'I heard at the wedding on Saturday night that Steve had been telling people in the village how you'd stolen a family heirloom . . . '

'The famous ring,' Rosalie protested. 'He inherited it from his grandmother and when we got engaged, he gave it to me. I did think in the midst of all the financial chaos that I would return it to him, but when I discovered he'd used funds from the business to buy a statement car and then disposed of the car without trace and with no money, not a single penny, coming back into the accounts, I decided I couldn't afford to be noble. I pawned it in Newcastle.' She pulled her mobile phone out of a pocket and dug slim fingers into the casing. It took a little manoeuvring, but a folded piece of paper slipped out. She sent him a speaking look and he felt this might be a make or break moment for them. He took the paper and unfolded it. The name along the heading wasn't a firm he knew, but he recognised the street and the area of Newcastle.

How did he feel about family heirlooms and their disposal? Well, he'd been trying to sell the house he'd inherited, hadn't he? It wasn't quite on the same personal level as a grandmother's ring, though.

'So that's where it is. I spoke to Mr Baxter senior and discovered he's not much worried except that he feels Steve is fixated on it and it might, just might, help his fight against the drink, if he had it back.' David paused and tried to work out how Rosalie was accepting that news. 'If you pawned it, it can be recovered. How much was the valuation?'

'They gave me fifteen hundred pounds which I used to defray the final staff wages.' Rosalie shifted uneasily in her chair. 'The thing is that Steve insured the ring for fifteen thousand pounds. I don't know how he managed that. I would have thought any insurer would want a valuation.'

David whistled through his teeth. Fifteen thousand pounds!

'They would, but how many shifty characters has Steve encountered since he began drinking heavily?' David could see that Steve might find someone set up as jeweller who would oblige him with a dodgy valuation. 'So, he thinks you stole the ring whereas you think, and I can see why, that as he'd given it to you, it was yours to sell.'

'It's worse than that, David. Steve put everything into my name so he was free of liability. However, he suggested that I should lose the ring and claim on the insurance.' Rosalie sat up straighter clearly, to David's eye, still incensed by the memory. 'He wanted to turn me into a criminal.'

'To finance his drinking,' David said, horrified.

'He claimed it was to make a fresh start. If he could turn up at the office in decent clothes and persuade his doctor to say he'd had a breakdown, he thought the firm might take him back on.' David watched Rosalie shudder. 'I would never have tried the insurance scam, but when I saw the paperwork for the car, it hardened all my resolutions. He'd paid for it through one of the business's accounts in cash by forging my signature.'

'This car, did he crash it?'

'Who knows. He had it one week when he was still working but before he must have started on the final drinking den binges,' Rosalie said, and he could see the memories were cloudy. 'It is difficult to work it all out, but there was then a week when he had no car.'

'Did he report it missing? Make an insurance claim?'

'No, not as far as I know.'

'Which makes me think he was in a drink fuelled accident and couldn't involve the police without being arrested,' David said.

Rosalie sent him a look of such bleak agreement his heart tripped. 'By that stage, his father got involved and he was hauled off to rehab.' She sighed. 'I don't know, David. It's almost as though he regards the fifteen thousand pounds as a kind of talisman.'

'You aren't in a financial position to redeem the pawn?'

'Certainly not. I used my salary to make a payment to our lawyers because they were dunning Dad for it,' she said, and David was touched by the proud jut of her chin. She'd set out to repay this debt to her parents and she was doing it. However, he hoped to short-circuit a lot of that pain.

'And if you do redeem the pawn, or if someone did on your behalf, and gave the ring back to him . . . '

'He could put his plan of losing it and claiming on the insurance into action. He is fairly expert at forging my signature,' Rosalie said.

Really?' David mused. 'Was the insurance policy renewed year on year?'

'Oh!' David was happy to see the relieved smile that covered Rosalie's face. 'Oh, yes. It'll run out in two weeks' time, maybe less. And all the bank accounts were closed down, so it can't renew again. He'd have to start from scratch.'

* * *

Rosalie was weak with relief. Not only had she begun to repay her debt to her father, but David had shown her that Steve's remaining grip on her was about to become nothing more than smoke drifting from a fire long gone out.

'We should get back to the kitchen and see if it's still intact,' David said. Rosalie looked at him. Desire filled his gaze and its strength warmed her.

'Yes,' she said, shakily aware that they'd be leaving this oasis of calm for the bustle of the house and estate. 'On the other hand, I did set the timer. The oven will switch off automatically.' How amenable would David be to a detour, she wondered.

'I don't know what's going through that fertile brain of yours, Rosalie Garden, but whatever it is, stop. You're overthinking so hard there's a groove down the middle of your forehead,' David said. He leaned in and pulled her bodily up from the basket chair.

'Overthinking?' Rosalie felt the warmth of his body where they were touching. The contact was certainly making her overthink what might happen next.

'What?'

'Are you going to kiss me?'

'Oh yes. It's a good way to begin.'

Rosalie lifted her face to his and he brought his head down to kiss her. Gone was the indecision of their first encounter. David's hands slid down her slender back and tucked under her bottom to pull her hard into his body. She protested mildly as he pulled away.

'Not here, my love, not here,' David said. They stumbled back along the overgrown path and skirted the pond before reaching the courtyard and bringing on all the security lighting. David opened the door of the kennel and let Bracken slide in beside the other dogs.

He tugged her into the porch as he

fumbled for his keys and opened the door of the carriage house. They fell through it and stopped short in wonder.

'Mother's bedroom is on the other side,' David said and laughed.

'What's funny?' she asked.

'A man of my age worrying about whether his mother will have seen him arrive home with a beautiful and seductive woman.'

'I love your small talk,' Rosalie said, 'You could carry on with that.'

'I could, but it would get in the way of the other things we could be indulging in.' He paused, and Rosalie sensed the change in him. Surely, surely he wasn't going to turn her away again? She thought she might die of unrequited longing if he did.

'Other things?' she asked helpfully. 'You mean there's more than kissing?'

'Rosalie are you sure? You're not just . . . '

'Just what? Grateful that you've laid Steve's ghost. Oh, I'm sorry. That was a bad choice of words,' Rosalie stumbled to a halt. How could she have been so insensitive?

'Well, that's another thing. There is a ghost in my past, but you know about her and she's more of a wraith now, really. Only, I haven't been with anyone since . . . since Libby died.'

'Out of the way of it, are we?' Rosalie said, risking a joke to lighten the moment. 'Me, too. Maybe we could get back in the groove together.'

'I honestly think you've been spending too much time with those Doig twins,' David said, but they were the last words he spoke for some time.

The wall clock downstairs in David's kitchen struck two am and Rosalie stirred out of sleep. She turned over and slid off the bed onto the floor before padding around it to find her discarded clothes. Bundling them under one arm, she crept down the polished wood stairs until she felt the cold granite tiles underfoot. Stopping momentarily to pull on her track suit, she left the carriage house and sprinted for the back door of the mansion. Once inside, she leant back against the kitchen door and breathed slowly. A huge smile broke over her as she pushed away from the door and made for her rooms. Maybe she would have to leave for Newcastle in search of another job while the new owner got his business up and running, but surely, after their hours together tonight, David would follow her there?

Another smile broke as she realised that was a thought she wouldn't have had as recently as yesterday.

★ ★ ★

Rosalie was late down that morning and Betty and Wyn were already clearing up Agnes's breakfast.

'I am so sorry,' she said as she stumbled into the kitchen still trying to fix the toggles into her tunic. 'I don't know what happened, but I saw the time at five-thirty and then again ten minutes ago.

'So you say,' Betty said in aggrieved tones that could have been real, but could just as easily be a wind-up. 'It's as well that I know how to present a fruit medley with aplomb . . . '

'Would that be aplum?' Wyn asked and they burst into fits of laughter.

'Really, I am sorry . . . '

'Lighten up, lovey,' Wyn said. 'Mrs L wasn't looking very fresh herself this morning. I blame Alastair Craig.' They heard Bracken's excited bark outside, and realised Agnes was crossing the yard. Wyn shut the dishwasher, pressed the start button and headed out into the main house with Betty. Agnes came in then with Bracken at heel and sent Rosalie a broad grin. So much, Rosalie thought, for discretion. She had a distinct impression Betty and Wyn were up to speed on her romantic life, too.

'Sit down,' Agnes said, 'As your dinner was still in the oven this morning, I expect you're hungry,' in a tone that Rosalie knew didn't allow any argument. She sat and her boss served up breakfast.

'I do feel more human now, thanks, Agnes.' More human, she thought, and completely mortified. How could she have made such a 'teen in love and too blind to see anything obvious' mistake?

The thought of her hours with David made her feel alive and ready for all the challenges of her life in a way she hadn't experienced in a long, long time. Would he be working in the carriage house today, she wondered, or would he really have to go to Durham or Highmere?

'I saw David. He's gone off into Newcastle to deal with some business,' Agnes said without expanding.

That news dampened Rosalie's excitement, but then maybe he had a site in Newcastle, too. His work would be at different stages in different places. On the other hand, perhaps there was a more sinister reason for his trip.

'There was a man at the wedding on Saturday who expressed a very keen interest in buying your business,' Rosalie said tentatively. 'Has David perhaps gone to see him?'

'No, I don't think so,' Agnes said.

'Because it might be time to tell David

that Tam has no intention of starting a re-cycling works.'

'I think David worked that out, my dear. So, he knows, but you should discuss it with him,' Agnes said cryptically and refused to comment further. 'Rosalie, we, that is David and I, have taken a liberty . . .'

Rosalie was astonished by the embarrassed blush covering Agnes's face and neck. Just as she began to fear that they'd decided to let her go, a car turned into the back yard.

'Ah, too late. I did promise David I would have given you a little warning, but of course you slept late and now it's too late.' Agnes looked stricken.

'Rosalie, we have invited your parents to spend a few days here in the comparative calm after the wedding you've been working so hard on.'

Rosalie was speechless with shock.

The back door opened and David came in carrying a couple of suitcases. Rosalie knew he must have registered the shock on her face.

'Mother, you promised to give Rosalie some warning,' he said, but the accusation sat lightly, and he smiled at them both.

'The chef slept late,' Agnes said defensively. 'Besides, too much warning would have had her making their favourite lunch or something.'

Rosalie crossed the room and went out into the yard. She hardly believed David and Agnes had done this for her, but there her parents were looking round and fending off Bracken's hopeful attentions.

'Mum,' she said and wrapped her mother in a big hug.

'Dad.' She leant in for a kiss from her father, but with one eye on his walking stick had to forgo a hug.

'My dear,' her dad said, and Rosalie could see the unshed tears. 'How kind of the Logies to offer us this chance to see where you're going to be living.'

She didn't answer that because of course she would be leaving after the take-over in order to carry on earning without a break. It was a lowering thought and perhaps it showed in her face.

'Why so glum?' her dad asked. 'It must be such a relief to know Steve Baxter is back in Newcastle.'

'It certainly is.'

22

It was well into the afternoon before Rosalie was able to get some time alone with David. She crossed the courtyard and found the door of the carriage house open. She knocked and went in when David called.

'I've been hoping you'd come,' he said simply. 'Parents gone for a rest?'

'They have. Dad needs it as part of his recovery and Mum is just so tired from looking after him,' Rosalie said. It was heart-breaking to see her father relying so heavily on his walking aids, but she knew he was making good progress. It all took time.

'You look lovely in that colour,' David said. 'Burnt orange. It brings out all the highlights in your hair.'

'David, I've made such a mess of everything,' Rosalie said.

'I know. You gave all your trust to a practised conman who fooled a whole

HR department. You came up with two horrible ideas to prevent the sale of my house and save Mum's business. One of them foiled by Betty's housekeeping but the other enhanced by Tam Anscombe's divine comedy.'

'This is serious,' she said. 'You must listen.'

'On the other hand,' David said, ignoring her distress, 'you gave up your engagement ring to pay your staff.' He pulled a large brown envelope across the table beside him and upended it. A battered ring box fell out.

Rosalie pulled out her mobile phone and slid her fingers into the casing. It was empty. 'You kept the pawn ticket,' she whispered.

'I did. It seemed to me that you could return the ring to Steve's dad and let him decide what next,' David said quietly.

Rosalie nodded. 'It might be the best way.'

'And on the subject of your failings, we come to the way you rose to the challenge of feeding 150 people a five-star meal when your sous chefs had been replaced by an inexperienced amateur and an over-confident professional.'

'I can't say a word against either as they both did an amazing job,' Rosalie said with a grin.

'No, it was you who did the amazing job. It was you who pulled yourself together and re-organised, and then re-organised again and just got on with it. I think it augurs well for the business in the years to come,' David said.

'As to that, David, I don't think I can continue here when your man takes over.'

'Why not?'

'I can't have a gap in my earnings because I do need to repay Dad,' she said, but saw that he wasn't convinced. 'And I cannot stay on here when you're living across the yard.'

'I hoped that would be your reason, my darling girl. I've been a bit slow on the uptake, I feel.' He drew Rosalie closer and wrapped his arms around her. 'I tell myself that you are putting on a little weight, but you are still working too hard.'

'David . . .'

'And talking too much,' David said, and Rosalie smiled then before he kissed her.

'David, you must let me say thank you. It's so wonderful to have Mum and Dad here.'

'I thought you'd like it and it'll give them a chance to see if they like the area,' David said, and she was aware of his quizzical look.

'You're not selling up,' she said as she realised what it meant. 'You're going to keep the house.'

'I am going to keep the house. I think it began to dawn on me when we sat with Phemie Waugh in the garden that morning. She clearly enjoyed being here and the house seemed to welcome her.' David paused and Rosalie wondered if that was a catch in his voice. 'It has slowly crept up on me that I enjoyed giving her that peace. Maybe I'm never going to be an hotelier like Mum, but I think I will enjoy sharing the house with others. And if I can marry a really good chef, I might keep the business, too,' David said.

'What about Alastair Craig and the plans for a spa?'

'I really don't care,' David said, and kissed her again.

We do hope that you have enjoyed reading this large print book.

Did you know that all of our titles are available for purchase?

We publish a wide range of high quality large print books including:
Romances, Mysteries, Classics
General Fiction
Non Fiction and Westerns

Special interest titles available in large print are:
The Little Oxford Dictionary
Music Book, Song Book
Hymn Book, Service Book

Also available from us courtesy of Oxford University Press:
Young Readers' Dictionary
(large print edition)
Young Readers' Thesaurus
(large print edition)

For further information or a free brochure, please contact us at:
Ulverscroft Large Print Books Ltd.,
The Green, Bradgate Road, Anstey,
Leicester, LE7 7FU, England.
Tel: (00 44) **0116 236 4325**
Fax: (00 44) **0116 234 0205**

THE OTHER WOMAN

Wendy Kremer

Matthew faces a tough choice. Should he quit his job and take on the family firm? His girlfriend in London, Celia, definitely can't imagine living in the provinces, but Matthew knows the local community depends on the company for work. One of its employees, Kate, unintentionally helps him to accept the challenge. Kate likes Matthew, but he already has a partner, so he's off-limits. Will Matthew yield to Celia's demands?